"Squirrels."

Alida stared at him.

"Squirrels get into the attic and go down between the partitions. You heard squirrels. Believe me, there's nothing else in that room."

Alida felt her face flush. "Really, I—I'm very sorry—" she began.

"Only a stubborn idiot would want to be alone in that isolated old place," Justin said.

"I'm charmed with your opinion of me." She smiled sarcastically. "Nothing you can say will change my plans."

Alida told herself she'd be damned if she'd go to a motel, even if ten thousand squirrels invaded the house. They could line up at the foot of the bed and nibble on acorns while they watched her sleep, for all she cared. She'd show this opinionated, domineering man he couldn't order her around. He didn't own the mansion— or her, either!

Dear Reader,

Welcome to Silhouette! Our goal is to give you hours of unbeatable reading pleasure, and we hope you'll enjoy each month's six new Silhouette Desires. These sensual, provocative love stories are both believable and compelling—sometimes they're poignant, sometimes humorous, but always enjoyable.

Indulge yourself. Experience all the passion and excitement of falling in love along with our heroine as she meets the irresistible man of her dreams and together they overcome all obstacles in the path to a happy ending.

If this is your first Desire, I hope it'll be the first of many. If you're already a Silhouette Desire reader, thanks for your support! Look for some of your favorite authors in the coming months: Stephanie James, Diana Palmer, Dixie Browning, Ann Major and Doreen Owens Malek, to name just a few.

Happy reading!

Isabel Swift
Senior Editor

SDRL-7/85

DIANA STUART
The Shadow Between

Silhouette Desire
Published by Silhouette Books New York
America's Publisher of Contemporary Romance

SILHOUETTE BOOKS
300 E. 42nd St., New York, N.Y. 10017

Copyright © 1986 by Jane Toombs

Distributed by Pocket Books

ISBN: 0-373-05257-X

First Silhouette Books printing January 1986

10 9 8 7 6 5 4 3 2 1

America's Publisher of Contemporary Romance

Printed in the U.S.A.

Books by Diana Stuart

Sihouette Desire

A Prime Specimen #172
Leader of the Pack #238
The Shadow Between #257

DIANA STUART

lives in the Hudson River Highlands and has been publishing gothic and adventure romance novels since 1973. A nurse, she's fascinated with Indian culture. She is a native Californian.

One

Alida Drury caught her breath when she drove onto the dam and saw the dark green of the Catskills brooding over the shimmering gray-blue water. She'd forgotten the natural beauty of New York State once the city was left behind.

Alida smiled at her thought. Natural? The invitingly cool lake she admired was man-made. Ashokan Reservoir, storage for New York City water.

It was lovely all the same.

She drove her rented Citation across the bridge over the lake. Thunder King Mountain faced her, dwarfed by Slide Mountain and the higher Catskill peaks beyond. Clouds massed in the sky above them.

She wondered if she'd come this way with her mother sixteen years ago when she was ten. She didn't remember crossing the reservoir, she only remembered the greenery closing about the car as they climbed Thunder King, the leafy branches meeting overhead until she fancied they drove along the bottom of a lake under green water.

As she left the bridge, Alida flicked off the air conditioning and opened her window. When she turned onto the gravel road up Thunder King July sultriness flowed in. She smelled the aromatic scent of the pines set like rows of sentinels on both sides of the road. She saw a deer's head carved on a wooden sign to her right, where a private road branched off to vanish in the trees.

Alida nodded. Tomorrow she'd be turning into that road when she kept her appointment to meet David McLeod who was staying in a friend's hunting lodge at the foot of Thunder King.

As the grade grew steeper, the car automatically shifted down. The pines thinned, giving way to maples and other hardwoods so close to the road their branches brushed her car's top. There were no houses, for all the land on this side of Thunder King belonged to the McLeods. The heavily wooded slope was high enough to make a ski run feasible. That was one of the reasons Kentin Hotels Incorporated, KHI, wanted the McLeod estate.

And KHI was the reason she was here. Again, after all these years. Back to the spot she'd dreamed of since she was ten.

A week ago in Phoenix, where she lived and worked, her boss, Ken Hubbard, head of KHI's land acquisition division, had called her into his office.

"Didn't you say you'd actually stayed at the McLeod mansion when you were a child?" he'd asked.

"Well, yes," Alida told him, "but only for a month. My mother—"

Ken waved his hand, not interested in why she'd been there. "How'd you like to visit the place again?"

For a moment excitement crackled through Alida, then she eyed Ken narrowly. "You mean I'm to fly east with you?"

Ken shook his head. "I thought I'd let you try your wings. Go alone."

As she poured out her delighted acceptance, Alida decided she knew why Ken was sending her instead of going himself. He and his wife had planned a trip to Switzerland for July and he'd have to cancel it if he obeyed David McLeod's summons to meet with him in the upstate New York town of Persis.

"I want to sit down and talk to a representative of KHI face-to-face before I decide whether or not to sign the final papers," the owner of the McLeod estate had written.

Ken rose and came around his desk to stand beside Alida's chair. "I've already cleared your going in my place," he said. "Both David McLeod and the powers upstairs here have agreed."

"You must have been sure I'd want to go."

He grinned down at her. "I'm beginning to appreciate how your business-comes-first mind works."

Her new position as Ken's personal aid had given Alida problems for a while, but she'd parried his passes with unamused firmness until he was finally convinced their relationship was to be entirely confined to KHI affairs.

This New York trip would give her a chance to negotiate a deal by herself, even if it was in the final stages. She was certain her success—she wouldn't admit the possibility of failing—would encourage Ken to allow her more responsibility in the future.

Alida stood and faced him. "Thanks, Ken."

His smile faded. "I know you'll do fine. You've worked with me on this McLeod acquisition from the beginning. Hell, you know as much as I do about the possibilities there for the year-round recreation complex we have planned."

She nodded. Was he having second thoughts about not going himself?

"McLeod's a bit odd," Ken went on. "He's only in his mid-fifties, but he lives like an old hermit on that island he owns in Main. Widowed. Maybe not as loaded as a Rockefeller but he's got plenty. There's no financial need to sell the Thunder King estate."

"I've heard he never sets foot on it."

"Right. He definitely wants to sell. At least I think so. I hope this meeting with you is just one of his quirks. Use your Kentin know-how. Tactful but firm."

"Of course." Alida's tone was positive. It was just like Ken to decide she knew absolutely nothing about land acquisition now that he'd committed her to taking his place. "I can handle it," she went on. "Don't worry. Enjoy Switzerland."

"I wouldn't let you go if I didn't think you could do it, Switzerland or not." He'd hesitated, then added, "For God's sake don't make any of your leaping assumptions. Facts, Alida. Stick to facts and we'll be home free."

All thoughts of Ken faded from Alida's mind when she saw the round stone tower thrusting above a tangle of maple branches. The gatehouse! She slowed the car, signaling a left turn. Avoiding a particularly deep pothole as she turned into the dirt drive, Alida noted that KHI would have to resurface the road completely; it obviously hadn't been maintained.

A heavy chain, stretching between stone pillars, blocked her way. She stopped the car. There was no trace of the iron gates she remembered nor of the sign reading McLeod in ornate lettering.

Alida glanced to the right. KHI's survey engineer had reported someone living in the stone gatehouse. Alida touched the horn lightly, watching to see if anyone came out. As a child she'd loved the small stone cottage with the round tower almost as large as the rest of the building.

"It's the old witch's house," she'd told her mother. "But don't worry, Hansel and Gretel already pushed her into the oven and so she's dead." Alida grimaced, remembering. Fairy tales could be quite violent.

Apparently no one was home, so she got out of the car and walked to the chain. As she reached for the hook that held it to the pillar she saw movement near the gatehouse and turned.

A gray-haired woman limped toward her along a stone path that went through a rose garden between the gatehouse and the drive. Sweeter than any hot-house roses, the scent of the flowers drifted to Alida on the warm breeze. Despite the heat, the old woman wore a long black dress.

"I'm from Kentin Hotels...." Alida began. Her words trailed away as the woman stopped abruptly, gazing at her with what appeared to be horrified recognition.

She can't know me, Alida thought in confusion. I've never seen her before in my life.

When she was a child a gnarled, bewhiskered caretaker had lived in the gatehouse. Alone. Who was this old woman?

The woman turned and hobbled back toward the house.

"Wait!" Alida called. "I'm from Kentin Hotels. Mr. McLeod has arranged for me to stay at the mansion."

The woman hurried on, paying no attention to her, and disappeared inside the gatehouse, shutting the door behind her with a bang.

Alida shrugged and reached for the chain, unhooked it and hauled the links clear of the drive. She got in the car and, after driving past, stopped to rehook the chain. This was going to be a bother if she drove in and out very often. She returned to the car and started the long winding climb to the McLeod mansion.

Once this road had viewpoints where the trees had been cut and thinned so those coming to the house could see the valley below, see the water of the reservoir glittering in the sun, and the steeples of Persis eight miles away. Now saplings crowded the old clearings—ash, maple, birch—blocking the view.

The rest of the trees were ancient giants forming a tunnel of green barely wide enough for the car. She crossed a stone bridge over a small stream, made a looping turn and climbed higher, recrossing the same stream over another bridge.

Alida's anticipation mounted as she looked eagerly ahead for her first glimpse of the white columns supporting the wide veranda that ran halfway around the mansion. Unlike the gatehouse, the main house was wooden, a rambling, multichimneyed, three-story structure, white with dark green shutters. At ten she'd thought it the most beautiful house she'd ever seen.

"We'll raze it," Ken had told her. "Our architect says it's a monstrosity."

Alida's car rounded the last curve and the old mansion appeared before her. She stepped on the brakes and gasped, not in delighted recognition but in distress.

She'd known the house hadn't been occupied by the McLeods since shortly after her visit here as a child, but the family had hired caretakers to live in an apartment made from three downstairs rooms. The couple had lived there until about two years ago. Surely the proud old house couldn't have deteriorated so much in such a short period of time.

The wooden siding was sadly in need of paint, many of the boards were weathered gray and much of the veranda sagged alarmingly. Some of the shutters hung by one hinge, others were gone altogether; shingles angled askew on the roofs and several of the chimneys had bricks missing.

Tears came to Alida's eyes. Why had the McLeods neglected this once gracious and lovely home? It couldn't be lack of money—as Ken had pointed out, David McLeod was a wealthy man. She blinked back tears as she tried to suppress burgeoning anger. She was here as an agent of KHI, not as Alida Drury. It was none of her business what David McLeod chose to do with his property as long as he sold it to her company.

David McLeod had agreed to let her stay in the caretaker's apartment for the week or so she'd be in the Catskills. When she'd made the request, she'd expected the house to be as it had been years before. If the apartment was anything like the house's exterior, she'd have to find a motel instead.

Alida parked under the porte cochere and got out. She dug into her bag for the keys Ken had given her and climbed the sagging steps to the front door. She stopped to look at the brass eagle knocker. Once shining, it was now dull and unpolished. She touched the oversized brass doorknob. To her surprise it turned easily and the door opened.

She hesitated before stepping inside. Had someone left the door unlocked in case she didn't have a key? Alida shook her head. Surely not. Yet she could hardly believe the house was left open all the time. She glanced behind her even though she knew the circular drive was empty and only her car was parked under the porte cochere.

The mansion was more than eight miles from Persis, the nearest town, and since the McLeods owned so much land there were no nearby neighbors. It wasn't likely someone had walked up here from Persis. Perhaps that old woman in the gatehouse had a key and had opened the door for her, though it was a long climb for an old woman, especially one who limped.

With anticipation mixed with apprehension as to what condition she'd find in the interior, Alida stepped over the threshold. In the foyer, the crystal chandelier with its trembling teardrops still hung above the foot of the winding staircase, but the prisms were heavy and dull with dust. The foyer was unfurnished, as was the dining room to her left.

She'd been told the caretaker's apartment was to the right. Alida turned and unlocked a door with the smaller of her two keys, passed along a short hallway and entered what her mother had called the morning room. She smiled in relief and pleasure.

The room was furnished as a living room and looked comfortable. The bare oak floors were clean. Many-paned oriel windows faced the front of the house where rose of sharon bushes struggled to survive the wild wood's growth that had crept threateningly close. She found that what had been the kitchen was partitioned off so that the back half was now a large and modern bathroom. In the kitchen half, an older-model refrigerator hummed efficiently.

The bedroom was at the side of the house. She thought it might once have been a servants' sitting room but she couldn't remember. The bed hadn't been made, so she could tell the mattress and springs were new. Fresh bed linen was piled on the chest of drawers.

She'd be quite comfortable here, Alida decided. There was no need to look for a motel. She hated the sterility of motels. Besides, she really wanted to stay at the mansion. Ever since she'd been a child she'd dreamed of returning here one day. Not exactly under these circumstances, but at least it was a dream come partly true.

Alida walked back through the apartment into the foyer, eager to revisit the rest of the mansion. As she passed the stairs, she noticed a dark red rose on the flat newel post and nodded. It must have been the gatehouse woman who'd opened the house and cleaned the apartment. She walked under an archway and passed between the open double doors into the library.

Dust lay thick on the empty bookshelves. The big room suddenly grew dark and Alida realized a cloud had covered the sun. She remembered the thunderheads over the peaks and thought a storm would be a welcome relief after the hot and humid day.

Alida closed her eyes, picturing the empty library as it had once been: A vast and gleaming mahogany desk in front of the long windows looking out onto a small orchard. A high mahogany table where her mother perched on a tall stool to appraise leather-covered books with gilt lettering on their spines and covers. She could almost see the sparkle in her mother's dark eyes when she held up a book for Alida to see.

"Lida, darling," her mother would cry, "look at this. See where Mr. Irving has autographed his book. Do you know how rare this is? Yet I doubt if anyone has ever bothered to read the story. A shame—such a beautiful book, inside and out."

Ten-year-old Alida couldn't imagine anyone having books and not reading them. Even today, she still didn't understand such people. She sighed, missing her mother, dead two years now—more than mother and daughter, they'd been friends.

"What are you doing here?" a man's voice demanded.

Alida's eyes flew open and she whirled to stare at the doorway. A tall broad-shouldered man stood glaring at her from angry amber eyes. He looked no older than thirty and his golden hair curled low on a neck that was tanned to the same golden brown as his eyes.

A shock of recognition jolted through Alida. She'd seen this handsome man before, she was certain. In a moment she'd recall where.

"Well?" he said curtly.

Alida gathered her wits. "I'm Alida Drury. I came...that is, I'm here—"

He waved his hand, cutting her off. He took a step toward her. "I've never heard of you." His mouth twisted. "Don't bother trying to think up a story about why you're in this house. I've heard enough lies from your kind."

"But I—" she protested.

He took two quick strides and grasped her shoulders. She gazed into his furious eyes, unable for a moment to think, much less speak. His hands were only on her shoulders but she felt his touch throughout her entire body.

"I know damned well why you're here," he growled, shaking her. "You've sneaked into the house to search for the diamonds."

Alida stared at the golden man towering over her. A memory flashed through her mind of being ten, of waiting at the long library windows for a glimpse of the tanned and laughing teenaged boy she'd secretly named after the sun god in her Greek mythology book.

Other boys raced after him, following him across the lawns and through the woods, but he was always the leader, a shining and golden Apollo.

"You're Justin McLeod!" she exclaimed.

He blinked, his amber eyes momentarily puzzled, and his grip on her shoulders eased. Alida's heart pounded as she stared at his hard-planed face so close to hers, at his generous mouth, sensitive and inviting, a mouth that belied the angry glint in his eyes.

She didn't understand why he was so furious. What was it he'd said about diamonds? She'd have to stop behaving as if she were still ten years old and take control of the situation.

Alida jerked from his grasp. "I told you who I was," she said, marveling at how crisp her voice sounded. "Alida Drury from Kentin Hotels. Surely you knew I was coming to see your father."

His jaw tightened and he took a deep breath. "I knew Kentin was sending a representative, yes. Ken Hubbard, I believe the name was." His words were terse with annoyance.

Alida felt a dart of irritation. After all, she was here at David McLeod's request. "Mr. Hubbard sent me in his place. As he notified Mr. David McLeod. Mr. McLeod had no objection."

Justin's face remained set and cold.

Alida's spark of annoyance grew as she watched his glance flick over her. "I'd like to have a look at the rest of the house if you don't mind," she told him.

"Why? Your company plans to tear it down. What difference does it make whether you see the rooms or not?"

She certainly wouldn't tell this rude and arrogant man why she wanted to explore the mansion. He didn't remember the lonely little girl who trailed after him for part of one summer—why should he? Alida touched her shoulder-length black hair. She was no longer a child, there was nothing to link her with that ten-year-old in anyone's mind.

Raising her eyebrows, she shrugged. Anger seethed inside her but she did her best to appear cool and disdainful. It was a matter of complete indifference to her whether Justin showed her through the house or she made her own way about the mansion. She'd turn away. Walk out of the library. Go to the apartment and wait for him to leave.

She didn't move. It was as though Justin were the sun and she a sunflower destined to be drawn to his golden shining. She found herself wondering what it would be like to run her fingers over the fascinating curve of his lips.

Alida swallowed and stood straighter. What on earth was the matter with her? She'd learned long ago how to handle such feelings. They had no place in business, none at all. Hadn't she managed to convince Ken, infamous all through KHI for his womanizing, that she'd be his business associate only?

She was at the McLeod mansion on business.

"The upstairs isn't in good condition," Justin said abruptly. "Watch your step." He turned on his heel and strode from the library, leaving her staring after him. From the foyer Justin glanced around at her. "Well? I thought you wanted to be shown through the house."

She started toward him, clenching her teeth to keep back a furious reply. When he saw she was coming, he walked on to the stairs. Fuming, she followed him.

The long curve of the staircase was still impressive though the walnut banisters, their rail, and the newel post no longer gleamed with polish, and the treads were worn and dusty.

"The carpeting?" Alida asked, recalling how the stairs used to be covered with a lovely Aubusson.

"The worn edges were a hazard," Justin snapped. "We had the carpet ripped up."

The dark oak of the upstairs floors, bare like the downstairs, showed footprints crisscrossing the dust. The corridors were gloomy and smelled of old wood. Justin flung open the doors as they passed to reveal one empty bedroom after another.

Alida saw the bedroom she'd shared with her mother, turning her head away from the sight of the rose-latticed wallpaper hanging in strips, and becoming more and more depressed with this trip into the past. What had she expected to find?

She was ready to tell Justin she'd seen enough when he passed by a door without opening it. Alida stopped, curious.

"What's in there?" she asked.

"I don't have the key to Priscilla's room but it's empty, like all the rest."

"Do you mean this room is locked?"

He nodded curtly.

"But why lock an empty room?"

"Why not?" His tone was icy. He moved on to the next door. "This leads to the attic. It's also empty."

"I'll take your word for it." She'd lost all desire to explore.

Justin paid her no heed, opening the attic door. As Alida stared up the dark, steep steps, she heard a faint rumble of thunder. She'd never been in the attic of the mansion and had no wish to see it now.

"I'll go first to make sure the stairs are safe." Justin's words might indicate concern, but the tone of his voice implied that it would serve her right if she broke her neck.

Alida hoped David McLeod wouldn't prove to be as difficult as his son. She ought to go back downstairs and leave Justin alone in the attic. Instead she started up the staircase, telling herself it was part of her job to finish inspecting the house. Just as it was to be polite to Justin McLeod, no matter how he acted.

The still air under the roof was hot and oppressive. Shadows were gathering between the chimneys and in the far reaches of the empty attic. Thunder rolled again, closer now, and through the small octagonal windows she saw storm clouds covering the sky. Alida thought this was the last place she'd choose to be on this stifling afternoon but, perversely, she walked past Justin, making a pretense of looking around. A floorboard tilted under her foot, she lost her balance, stumbled and began to fall.

Strong arms caught her, bringing her upright. For a moment her body was pressed against the length of Justin's. Alida drew in her breath. He smelled of maleness, a scent uniquely his tingled along her nerve endings. When he set her firmly on her feet, letting her go, she was shocked to realize she'd wanted him to hold her longer against the disturbing heat of his body.

"Thank you," she murmured, turning away to give her skirt an unnecessary brushing, hoping he hadn't noticed her breathlessness.

"I told you to watch your step," he said. "Have you had enough?"

Thunder rattled the leaded panes in the octagonal windows, startling her. Her hair hung damply to her neck in the stifling air. Yes, she'd had more than enough.

Of the attic and of Justin McLeod.

As she started for the stairs, she eyed the floorboards carefully to prevent tripping again. A bit of white caught her glance, something sticking between two of the unpainted boards. She crouched to pluck at it and teased a rectangle of paper from the crack.

It was a photograph, yellowing with age, of a darkly attractive young woman whose hair was swept up in the front in the pompadour popular during World War II. Alida stood and held out the snapshot to Justin.

He looked at it, then thrust her hand away. "I don't want any pictures of her," he said. "If it hadn't been for her..." He broke off, scowling.

Alida, puzzled, turned over the picture. There was writing on the back and though the ink was faded by time she made out a name, "Priscilla," and a date, "1942."

"The Priscilla whose room is locked?" A moment later she regretted her words since it was really none of her business. "I'm sorry," she added. "I don't mean to pry."

"As far as the McLeods are concerned, there was only one Priscilla." Justin stared from the face in the photograph to Alida. His eyes narrowed.

She swallowed, made apprehensive by his intent regard. For the first time she became conscious of the fact she was alone in this decaying mansion with Justin. The man was a stranger, really, no matter how she had fantasized about him as a child.

Before she could move, Justin stepped forward and gripped her chin between his thumb and forefinger, turning her face toward the window near the stair. A pulse pounded in her throat as she gazed into his eyes, eyes that glowed in the gray gloom of the attic as though lit from within.

Did he mean to kiss her?

The thought sent shivers of anticipation along her spine. A tingling began inside her, a desire to be held close to him. She'd never seen, never met a man to compare with Justin McLeod. He was as tawny and lithe as a cougar. Perhaps as dangerous. At this moment she didn't care.

Justin shook his head and his hand dropped from her face as he stepped back. "I'm getting as bad as he is," he muttered.

Alida had no idea what he meant. She felt bereft, then angry, thinking he must have seen what she expected, must have known she'd hoped he'd kiss her. Is that why he hadn't? Her face flamed.

Thunder growled, farther away now. She would have fled if Justin hadn't stood between her and the stairs. She was all too conscious of her travel-weary suit and heat-limp hair. She grew angrier when she thought of how disheveled she must look.

"I'd like to go down to my apartment," she snapped. "If you don't mind."

"Do you mean...?" He broke off. After a moment he added, "You can't stay in this house."

Her heart sank. Was Justin using the apartment? She hadn't noticed any sign of it but he could be. That meant she'd have to find a motel, much as she preferred not to. She'd looked forward to having the McLeod mansion for her own, if only for a short time.

"There must be a misunderstanding," she said. "I thought I had your father's permission to use the apartment."

"Damn it, the house is too isolated for a woman to stay in alone. There's not even a phone."

She'd been mistaken, Justin wasn't using the apartment. Alida smiled frostily. "I enjoy being by myself." She emphasized the last two words.

He glared at her. "Why the hell didn't Hubbard come himself? Trust a woman to foul things up."

Alida was speechless with indignation.

"Look, Ms. Drury," Justin said, "this is no place for a woman. This spring my father asked me to fly in from California because of repeated problems with trespassers breaking in. There hasn't been a caretaker living in the house for almost two years."

"I imagine word got around that the mansion was empty," Alida pointed out. "My car will be parked in front and I'll be careful to leave lights on so it'll be obvious someone's staying here." She spoke more positively than she felt. Nothing had been said about trespassers. Nor about not having a phone, for that matter.

"It's out of the question," Justin told her.

If she didn't stay here she'd be in a motel. "How long since the break-ins?"

"April. But—"

"Did the local police catch anyone?"

"Well, yes, the Persis police chief seemed to think they'd solved the problem."

"Then the trespassers are accounted for."

"The year before—"

She threw up her hands. "I don't want to hear about last year. All I want to do is go downstairs and rest."

"You can't stay here alone." He fired the words at her like bullets.

"Your father gave me permission to use the apartment. I am alone. I intend to remain alone. Here," Head high, she dared him to contradict her.

After a moment he shrugged. "I suppose if worse comes to worst, Mrs. Danford has a phone."

"Who?"

"In the gatehouse."

"And does Mrs. Danford live by herself?" Alida inquired sweetly.

He nodded.

"If she manages, old as she is, I'm sure I'll survive for a week or two."

"I wish you hadn't come here."

"That's evident."

"You don't understand—" he began.

"I think I understand quite well. It's clear you don't believe a woman can take care of herself, business-wise or otherwise. You're far behind the times, Mr. McLeod." Alida glanced down at the photograph in her hand. "Back in the forties with Priscilla."

His hand shot out and fastened on her wrist, making her drop the picture. She gasped in surprise.

"Damn it, don't mention her name!" he shouted. "I've heard enough about Priscilla. If it hadn't been for Priscilla, you wouldn't be standing here. You wouldn't be in my father's house."

Justin let go of her wrist, wheeled and ran down the stairs. Alida heard him descend to the first floor and heard the door slam. She was alone in the McLeod mansion, just as she'd insisted she wanted to be.

Only now she wasn't so certain she'd been right.

Two

───

The shadows in the attic thickened, crept closer. The stairwell was a dim abyss at Alida's feet. Without thinking, she looked for a light switch, then remembered the electricity for the house had been disconnected except for the apartment downstairs.

She'd never been afraid of the dark. She told herself she wasn't afraid now, but it would be wise to make her way down these steep stairs before daylight faded altogether.

On the second floor, she paused outside the room with the rose-trellised wallpaper, went in and crossed to the window. There was no sign of the green velvet back lawn that had once sloped to the trees. Between straggly patches of grass, saplings, mountain bushes and weeds fought each other in a desperate struggle for survival.

Alida glanced at the snapshot she'd picked up. Priscilla. Priscilla McLeod? Justin hadn't mentioned her last name. She'd been young and pretty in 1942, whoever she was. Today she'd be middle-aged, getting old.

Something about Priscilla's dark attractiveness reminded Alida of early pictures she'd seen of her mother.

"Dark as gypsies, Lida, both you and me," her mother had often said with a laugh. "Maybe that's why we never stay in one place."

This room with the rose-trellised wallpaper had been Alida's and her mother's for the time they stayed at the McLeod mansion. Alida sighed. She'd loved her mother, and they'd been close. Yet she'd never told her how, when she was a child, she'd longed for a home of their own. Her mother's job as an appraiser for a nationwide auction firm had sent them all over the country. The position paid well, they'd always been comfortable, but living in one apartment after another, they'd never had a real home.

Her first sight of the McLeod mansion had thrilled ten-year-old Alida. By the second day she'd begun to create a fantasy about the house belonging to her. It would be a home that, no matter how many times she left, would always be waiting for her. A home of her own, beautiful and never-changing. Waiting.

But the house *had* changed. And it never would belong to Alida Drury. As soon as KHI acquired the property, the house would be razed to make room for the inn and headquarters building of the resort complex.

Alida sighed and turned away from the window. As she stepped into the corridor, she heard a scratching sound and cocked her head to listen. Where was it coming from? She retraced her steps along the corridor, stopping outside one of the closed doors.

The door to Priscilla's room.

Tentatively she tried the knob. The door didn't open. It was locked, as Justin had told her.

She heard the noise again, and now she was certain it came from inside the room. Not exactly a scratching, she couldn't quite define the sound she heard. Was it something moving? Hair rose on the nape of her neck.

"Hello?" she said softly.

The sound stopped.

"Is anyone there?" she asked, louder.

No answer. No sound from behind the door.

In the gloom of the corridor, Alida stood listening but all around her the house was quiet. She stared at the locked door. Was Priscilla inside, waiting, listening as she was, waiting for her to leave? Alida shivered.

She stepped back, shaking her head angrily, annoyed with herself. The room was empty. Justin McLeod had said so.

Could she believe him? Why was he so against her staying in the apartment? And why was an empty room kept locked?

If it really was empty.

The noise came again and she took another step backward. She'd have to sleep in the apartment without knowing for certain that she was alone in the house. She knew she'd never close her eyes if she had to wonder what might be inside this locked room.

Alida hurried down the main staircase to the first floor and walked quickly out the front door. She skirted the house until she came to the back. Once trellised honeysuckle and trumpet vines had climbed the walls here, but the trellises had rotted and collapsed and the surviving vines twined untidily through bushes and around saplings. No trees grew close to the side of the mansion—the noise couldn't have come from a branch scraping against the wall or the windows.

She peered up at the second-story windows. All the panes, including those in Priscilla's room, were intact, so no bird could have flown through a broken window into the room. Her gaze went on up to the roof, and she eyed the many chimneys. No chimney broke the roofline near any of the back bedrooms.

Yet she was certain that whatever was causing the sounds was inside the locked room. How had it gotten in? Alida took a deep breath. She had no way of finding out unless she had a key—or an explanation from the McLeods.

She must find Justin and demand one or the other.

Perspiration trickled between her breasts—such a hot, humid day. She glanced hopefully at the sky, but the clouds had thinned and drifted apart. The storm had passed over without dropping rain on Thunder King Mountain. Alida glanced at her watch. Seven o'clock. She headed for her car.

As the Citation jounced downhill, Alida noticed the imprint of horseshoes in the dirt road. No wonder she hadn't seen a car parked near the mansion when she first arrived: Justin must have come on horseback.

A memory flashed before her—a much younger Justin galloping across the back lawn on a horse as black as night with a girl following him astride a palomino, her hair flying in the wind, hair as fair and light as dandelion fluff.

How Alida had longed to be that girl!

She compressed her lips. All that was in the past. Alida Drury trailed after no man. She certainly didn't intend to make an exception for the arrogant Justin McLeod.

When she reached the gatehouse she saw Mrs. Danford puttering among her roses. The garden was especially lovely, with not a dead bloom anywhere. The reds and pinks of the roses seemed to glow in the early evening light, their sweetness pouring into the car's open window.

"Your roses are gorgeous," Alida called to the old woman when she got out to unhook the chain. As she spoke, she remembered the dark red rose on the newel post.

The flower had been gone when she came back downstairs. No doubt Mrs. Danford had left it for Justin.

"I take good care of my roses," Mrs. Danford said. "Good care." She eyed Alida warily but her earlier shock wasn't evident.

"I can see you do." Alida dragged the chain aside, then added, "I'm coming back shortly so I'll leave the chain unhooked until then."

Mrs. Danford shrugged, saying nothing as she watched Alida get back into the car.

What upset her when she first saw me? Alida wondered. Maybe living in such an isolated spot had affected Mrs. Danford. A couple of weeks by yourself might be wonderful, but living alone here all year round was something else again.

The turnoff to the hunting lodge was near the foot of the mountain, and Alida drove up the private road a few yards, before stopping the car. Was this wise? She'd rushed down intending to confront Justin without considering what she might find at the lodge. For one thing, he might not be there. She would then have to talk to David McLeod, assuming he was in, for she was determined to find out about that locked room before spending the night in the apartment.

She expected David would be there since he'd been described as a recluse. Would her appearance this evening in any way jeopardize the sale of the estate to KHI?

She couldn't think why. At the worst, Mr. McLeod might consider her a bit silly to be frightened by a noise in a locked room.

Well, was she? Away from the mansion it was easier to dismiss what she'd heard, but she knew once she went back she'd be alone in the house listening for unexplained sounds. So, she was a bit frightened. What was wrong with that?

It would be easy enough for either of the McLeods to give her a key to the room, wouldn't it? For the noise *had* been inexplicable. Unless one of them could give her an explanation.

Alida shifted gear and went on, easing the car along the narrow curving drive. Again the trees closed overhead, surrounding her with green gloom.

The hunting lodge crouched under giant maples, their size making the building seem smaller than it was. The central part rose two stories with single-story wings at right angles on either side. At a guess the lodge had six bedrooms, Alida judged. All with their own bathrooms judging from the number of the roof vents. A luxurious hunting lodge. Well, of course, she hadn't expected to find the McLeods staying in a one-room log cabin.

She parked and climbed plank steps to a knotty pine door. When she touched the bell she heard the first few bars of "John Peel" sound inside.

A stocky man in navy-blue shirt and pants opened the door. As she was deciding he couldn't possibly be David McLeod, he said, "May I help you?" He spoke with a slight foreign accent she couldn't place.

"I'm Alida Drury," she told him. "Is Justin McLeod here?"

"I'm sorry, Ms. Drury, he is not."

"David McLeod, then."

The man hesitated. "I'll have to see if—"

"Who is it, Knowles?" a voice asked.

Knowles turned his head. "A Ms. Drury, sir."

Alida heard a sigh. A man appeared behind Knowles, taller, with gray-streaked dark hair. He wore a wine shirt and white pants. She was certain he was David McLeod but she'd understood he was in his late fifties and this sallow-faced man looked older. He didn't resemble Justin.

"Come in," David McLeod said. "Come in, Ms. Drury. I didn't expect you until..."

His words trailed of as she stepped past Knowles, who shut the door and left them. Alida began to explain why she'd come, but stopped in astonishment when she saw David's expression.

All the color had drained from his face. He stared at her as though she were an unwelcome ghost. "No," he muttered. "Oh my God, no."

"Mr. McLeod!" she exclaimed. "Is something wrong?"

He raised a trembling hand as though to ward her off. "Priscilla," he whispered.

Alida looked around for Knowles, wanting to ask for help, but he'd disappeared. She bit her lip, uncertain of what to do. Should she leave? Run to find Knowles?

The front door flew open and Justin McLeod strode into the entrance hall. He looked at his father, then scowled at Alida. He stepped between them.

"What have you said to him?" Justin demanded. "What have you done?"

Alida twisted her hands together. Obviously she'd upset David, but she hadn't meant to. She took a deep breath and let it out slowly.

"I don't know what's the matter," she said. "He invited me in and then something happened. All he said was, 'Priscilla.'"

"I was afraid of that," Justin growled. He turned his back to her and spoke to his father. "Look, Dad, it's all right. Come into the living room. You need to sit down."

"Who... who is she?" David asked weakly.

"She's Alida Drury from Kentin Hotels." Justin helped his father from the hall and as they went through an archway, Justin turned and jerked his head toward the front door.

Alida shrugged. She had no choice but to leave.

"Where is she?" Alida heard David ask as her hand touched the doorknob. "Have her come in here. No, Justin, don't fuss over me, I'm all right. I want to talk to that young woman."

A moment later Justin appeared in the archway. "Please come into the living room, Ms. Drury," he said coldly.

Alida walked into a room where deer heads on the walls stared glassy-eyed at the rifles and shotguns in glass-fronted walnut cases. Leather couches and chairs furnished the room. David was sitting in a lounger with his head back and feet up.

"Sit down, if you will," David told her.

Alida perched on a straight chair, the pungent scent of leather surrounding her.

For long moments no one spoke.

"I apologize for arriving here without warning," Alida said finally to David. "A problem came up at the mansion that I felt couldn't wait until our appointment tomorrow."

David waved his hand and she took it to mean it was all right that she'd come.

"What problem?" Justin demanded.

"There's something in that locked room you said was empty. I heard it."

Justin, who'd been standing beside his father, strode to her chair and glared down at her. "Are you deliberately trying to cause trouble?" he growled.

Alida bristled. "Certainly not!"

"Let the girl alone, Justin," David said. "Are you speaking of Priscilla's room?" he asked Alida.

"Yes. The room on the second floor that's locked. Justin told me it was empty but I heard scratching sounds inside."

"She shouldn't be in the mansion anyway," Justin said to his father. "It's no place for a woman to stay by herself."

"I don't mind being there alone," she put in, "but I do want an explanation of—"

Justin bent over her. "If you don't mind being in the mansion alone, then why did you run to my father the moment you heard a board creak? This settles it, you can't stay there."

"I didn't hear a creaking board!"

"Squirrels," David said.

Both Alida and Justin stared at him.

David eased the lounge chair upright and leaned forward. "Squirrels get into the attic and go down between the partitions. You heard squirrels, Ms. Drury. Believe me, there's nothing else in that room."

Alida felt her face flush. She had no doubt David's explanation was correct. She'd never lived in a house with squirrels in the attic, but she should have thought of such a possibility before rushing here to disturb David McLeod.

"Really, I . . . I'm very sorry—" she began.

"No harm done," David assured her. The color had returned to his face.

"Earlier this year I stayed a few nights at the Ashokan West Motel in Persis," Justin said to Alida. "It's quite comfortable."

Alida, who'd been smiling at David, turned to look at Justin. Her brows drew together. "Thank you for the recommendation, but I have no plans to move to a motel. I assure you I won't let squirrels in the partitions upset me again."

"I don't want you in the mansion!" Anger simmered in Justin's voice. His glance raked over her and once again she realized she wore wrinkled clothes. "Only a stubborn idiot would want to be alone in that isolated old place," he added.

"I'm charmed with your opinion of me." She smiled sarcastically. "Nothing you can say will change my plans."

Alida told herself she'd be damned if she'd go to a motel even if ten thousand squirrels invaded the house. They could line up at the foot of her bed and nibble on acorns while they watched her sleep for all she cared. She'd show this opinionated, domineering man he couldn't order her around. He didn't own the mansion—or her, either!

"Really, Justin, I did give Ms. Drury permission to stay in the caretaker's apartment," David said. "What difference can it make if she does?"

Alida grew warm with embarrassment. In her fury at Justin she'd completely forgotten his father. What must David think of her? Here she was, an agent of KHI, quarreling with his son.

"Thank you for allowing me to use the apartment," she managed to say.

"If you don't mind, Ms. Drury, I'd like to put off our appointment until the day after tomorrow," David said. "Does that suit you?"

"Yes, of course." Alida rose from her chair. Looking at David, she thought he seemed tired, perhaps ill. She hoped she hadn't upset him too much. Had he really thought she was Priscilla? How strange. Still, he seemed to be in command of himself now.

"I'll see you to your car," Justin said curtly.

To make certain I leave? she was tempted to ask.

Justin ushered her from the living room, opened the front door for her and walked beside her down the steps.

"I'm sure I can find my way from here," Alida said scathingly.

He paid no attention, walking to the car with her and opening the door. As she brushed past him to slide into the driver's seat, he gripped her arm, forcing her to turn toward him. He put his hands on her shoulders and stared down at her.

In the gathering dusk, his eyes were as yellow as candle flames. The anger smoldering in their depths was mixed with another emotion, one that made her heart quicken in response, preventing her from pulling away. Her gaze fastened on the tender curve of his lips, the only soft feature in the hard planes of his face. The curve tantalized her. His lips were so close. Tongues of flame licked at her, spreading fire throughout her body.

No man had ever affected her so acutely. She knew she should move away from his touch, but an invisible bond held her where she was as much as his hands on her shoulders did. Though still angry at Justin, she couldn't deny the sizzle of electricity leaping between them.

She caught her breath as she saw the pupils of his eyes dilate with the same desire that flickered inside her. How was it possible to be so furious with a man and yet crave his embrace?

Suddenly his hands slid down her shoulders to her arms. He thrust her into the car so abruptly she almost didn't duck fast enough to avoid hitting her head on the door frame. Before she could say a word he slammed the door shut, swung away, and strode toward the house without looking back.

Her emotions in a turmoil, Alida started the car. She fought the impulse to roar off, reminding herself the road was narrow and deer came out to feed at dusk. If she didn't pay strict attention to her driving, she might hit one. She'd had enough trouble today without courting further disaster.

All the way back up the mountain, Alida replayed the scene in the hunting lodge. Why was Justin so antagonistic to her? His father had been quite courteous once he'd gotten over the shock of her resemblance to Priscilla. Luckily the sale of the property to KHI depended on David, not Justin.

Or did it? Justin lived in California—perhaps he was here to try to prevent the transaction, to influence his father not to sell.

Alida clenched her teeth. Damn it, she'd fight Justin all the way if that was so. He'd implied he had no use for the old mansion, in which case his attitude would only be dog-in-the-manger.

And all that carrying on about her staying in the apartment. If David had given her permission, why should his son object? Unless he was afraid she'd discover something while staying there. He'd mentioned diamonds—what was that all about?

Alida shook her head as she stopped the car under the porte cochere. She got out and stared up at the dark bulk of the mansion outlined against the lesser darkness of the evening sky. Those were questions she had no answers for. More to the immediate point, she should have thought to leave a light on in the apartment.

Hearing the frogs shrill and the katydids complaining in their monotonous way, she realized an eastern country evening wasn't exactly quiet. Still, the absence of man-made sounds—the hum of traffic, sirens, the intrusive beat of other people's stereos—soothed her. There was nothing to fear in this peaceful setting.

Except her own inexplicable attraction to Justin McLeod. It must be a carryover from her childhood vision of him as Apollo. A young girl's dream, she told herself firmly. Both she and Justin were adults now, and such childish notions must be laid aside. The sale of the McLeod estate to KHI was why she was here, was what was important.

Forget Justin, she warned herself, ignore the excitement his presence evokes. Phoenix is full of attractive men, and you'll be back there in a few weeks.

Alida pulled a small flashlight from her shoulder bag and, carrying her suitcase, climbed the steps. She unlocked the front door, made her way across the foyer to the apartment, opened the door and flipped on the light switch. She shot the bolt before she went into the kitchen, wishing she'd thought to stock up on food—she'd had nothing to eat since noon. She was too tired to make the trip back down to Persis and so she'd have to go hungry until morning.

In the bedroom, she made the bed, then unpacked, laying out her nightgown, robe and slippers. Once she was ready for bed, though, Alida perversely felt wide awake. Rather than reading one of the several paperbacks she'd brought she decided to get out the agreement between KHI and David McLeod and go over the figures again.

Later, drowsy at last, she put aside the papers and crawled into the bed. Since she'd pulled down the shades, shutting off the bedside lamp plunged the room into absolute darkness, something she wasn't used to. In Phoenix outside lights reflected into her bedroom and it was never so dark she couldn't see anything.

Relax, she admonished herself. Go to sleep. Listen to the chorus of the frogs, the katydid choir. But her eyes stayed stubbornly open. After a few minutes she rose and turned on a light in the bathroom, leaving the door partly open. In no time at all she fell asleep.

Alida struggled back to consciousness, knowing something had awakened her. The night seemed very quiet, she didn't even hear the frogs now. She lay still, listening. There! What was it she heard? Footsteps? The noise was too faint for her to be certain.

She sat up, switched on the lamp and looked around the room. Everything was in order. Slipping into her robe, she searched the rest of the apartment and found nothing out of the ordinary. The bolts were secure on both the door to the foyer and the one that led from the kitchen to the side porch. There was nothing to worry about.

Should she look through the rest of the mansion? Alida frowned. The thought of exploring all those dark rooms, with only the beam of her tiny flashlight, definitely didn't appeal to her. No, what she heard was most likely David's squirrels. Either she must stop being nervous about staying here or give up and go to a motel.

And how Justin would laugh if she did.

When she returned to bed, his face stayed in her mind—the glow of desire turning his eyes to yellow fire, the sensual curve of his lips. The fit of his jeans and T-shirt had clearly shown his well-muscled body. McLeod was a Scottish name, wasn't it? She closed her eyes, imagining Justin in kilt and war bonnet, a Highland chief wielding his claymore in defense of Bonnie Prince Charlie, a champion of that wild, romantic cause.

Or Apollo, racing his sun chariot across the sky, commanding those dangerous fiery steeds he alone could control . . .

Stop it, Alida scolded herself. You're no longer ten years old, no longer a hero-worshipping child. She turned onto her side and resettled herself.

No, she wasn't a child, she was a woman. Unfortunately, that woman seemed to be as much in thrall to the adult Justin as ten-year-old Alida had been to the teenaged Justin. And that was the truth, like it or not.

I should never have come back to the Catskills, Alida thought. I'm afraid of what will happen if I see much more of Justin.

Three

Alida opened her eyes and saw light filtering through brown shades. Morning. Someone knocked at a door.

She rose, wrapped the robe about her and padded into the kitchen, calling, "Who is it?"

"Alida?" Justin's voice came from the side porch.

Her heart pounded as she approached the door. I should demand to know what he wants, she told herself. Ask him why he's waking me up so early.

Instead, she shot back the bolt and opened the door.

Justin stood on the porch wearing a blue T-shirt with his jeans. In one hand he held a package wrapped in green paper, in the other he carried a basket.

"May I come in?" he asked, smiling.

She stepped aside, watching him as he strode into the kitchen and set his package and basket on the formica-topped table. He whisked the green paper off and she gazed in surprise at five brown-eyed susans in a crystal bud vase.

"A peace offering," Justin murmured. "Somehow the brown-eyed susans remind me of you."

Disarmed, Alida looked from the golden flowers to Justin. The warmth in his voice and eyes speeded her pulse.

Justin lifted the top of the basket, and she breathed in the unmistakably delicious odor of freshly-baked bread. "I'll have breakfast on the table by the time you're dressed," he told her.

She flushed in dismay—again he'd caught her at a disadvantage. Her brown robe was modest enough, but utilitarian rather than pretty. She hated to think of how disheveled her hair must be after her restless night. Hurriedly she escaped to the bedroom.

When she came back into the kitchen, her dark hair, skimming her shoulders in soft waves, gleamed from the hurried brushing she'd given it. She wore a sleeveless red shirt with a divided skirt of blue denim and noticed his appreciative glance with satisfaction.

"Oh, wonderful!" she exclaimed, seeing the steaming mugs of coffee and the crusty rolls he'd set out on the table. "I'm truly starving—you're a lifesaver."

"Does this mean I'm forgiven?"

"How can I be angry at a man who brings me breakfast? Although it *is* a bit early."

His smile turned rueful. "That's right—you're just in from Phoenix, still operating on Mountain Time. Seems I'm destined to get off on the wrong foot with you, no matter what I do."

Alida touched one of the vivid golden petals of the brown-eyed susans, pleased by the contrast of the sturdy and bright roadside flowers and the delicate crystal vase.

"Your eyes are the same velvety brown as the centers of those flowers," he told her. "That was the first thing I noticed about you yesterday."

He was too close to her, making the breath catch in her throat. She raised an eyebrow. "The way you accused me of sneaking in to look for diamonds, I'm surprised you paid any attention to the color of my eyes. What did you mean about the diamonds, anyway?"

"You haven't heard of the McLeod diamond brooch?"

She shook her head.

"After that magazine article a few years back, I thought the entire country knew. I'll tell you about it while we eat." He sat down opposite her.

Alida felt more at ease with him across the table from her. She broke open one of the warm rolls and took a pat of butter. Justin sipped at his coffee and they sat for a few moments in companionable silence.

"The McLeod brooch is a family heirloom brought from Scotland over a hundred years ago. The market value would probably run to five figures today, so you can see why we've had trouble with trespassers trying to break into the mansion now that no one's living here."

"But why would anyone think the brooch might be here?"

"Because it's lost. Missing. My theory is that Stuart took the brooch when he disappeared; after all, it was technically his. At any rate, the diamonds have never been found. Over the years the house has been searched many times and so have the grounds, both by the family and by hired experts. To me that proves the brooch isn't here.'' He spread his hands. ''So Stuart has it. Wherever he might be.''

''I don't think I understand.''

''Stuart McLeod is the uncle I've never seen, my father's older brother. There were only the two of them. Father's convinced Stuart is dead. I don't know. It's true no one's seen Stuart since near the end of World War II.''

''So long ago. And he's never phoned nor written?''

''Nothing. He disappeared the night of the fire, when the Randolph house up the mountain burned to the ground. No connection, probably, but the fire fixed the night in my father's mind. He's nine years younger than Stuart and he was really just a boy when it all happened. The memories haunt him yet. The trouble began when Priscilla Tudor came to the McLeods as an English war orphan.''

''Priscilla.''

Justin picked up his coffee and took a sip, setting the mug down before he looked across the table at Alida. ''My father realizes now that except for your coloring and petiteness you don't really resemble Priscilla. He dwells on the past more than he ought to, and when you suddenly appeared last night you startled him.''

Alida bit her lip. ''I'm sorry I upset him. If I'd had any idea—''

''It's not your fault; how could you have known? I shouldn't have been curt with you but I worry about him. He hasn't been well.''

''Was Priscilla any relation to your family?''

Justin shook his head. "My grandfather knew her uncle, something like that. When she arrived that December, Stuart had just been discharged from the Air Corps after being wounded over Holland. My father says Stuart looked thin and limped a little but otherwise seemed fine. He was more or less engaged to a neighbor's daughter, Margaret Randolph. Her father's house was just over the ridge, I'll show you the ruins later."

"Randolph—the house that burned the night Stuart disappeared. Was Margaret hurt?"

"No one was injured in the fire but because of the general confusion, the family didn't realize Stuart and Priscilla were missing until late the next day."

Alida stared at him. "Priscilla disappeared, too?"

"Yes, they both left that night. Although Priscilla took some of her clothes, Stuart took nothing except what he was wearing. And the brooch. I've seen pictures of it—two circles of diamonds with a large single diamond in the center, the entire piece a bit larger than one of the older silver dollars. The brooch had been handed down in the McLeod family to the first-born son of each generation to give to his bride as a wedding gift. Which is why I'm convinced Stuart took it. For Priscilla."

"You say her name as though you dislike her. Have you ever met her?"

He shook his head. "Nothing was ever heard of Priscilla again. I suppose I've picked up my attitude from listening to my father. He's always blamed her for what happened, and keeps her room locked as though to shut away all trace of her."

"You can't lock away the past."

"Perhaps not. I've told you all this so you'll understand why I was so rude yesterday. You took me by surprise. I'm really quite harmless."

She gazed at him, saying nothing, thinking how wrong he was. Harmless! Didn't he know how attractive his combination of amber eyes, golden hair and tanned skin made him? Not to mention his superbly muscled body and his easy grace of movement. And that devastating smile. No man had ever affected her so potently in her entire life.

"I'll be a model of propriety from now on," he added with a one-sided grin. "To prove it, I'll show you around the property."

"I'd like that," she told him. It was why she was here—to secure the McLeod estate for her employers. If Justin cooperated, the path would be smooth and straight. She'd been a fool last night to worry about the sale.

As well as foolish to lose sleep over a possible involvement with Justin McLeod. She wouldn't be in New York long enough for anything to begin between them, even supposing that's what either of them wanted.

Justin led her into the woods behind the McLeod estate and along a faint path where the tall maples closed over their heads. Alida smelled the rich aroma of leaf mold, then the aromatic tang of pine as the hardwoods gave way to a stand of evergreens.

"This is a real forest," she said.

"'A weltering world of woods,' was how John Burroughs described the Catskills over a hundred years ago."

Alida remembered her mother reading to her from one of the great naturalist's books describing how whitetail deer bear their fawns in late May or early June. "Do you think we might see a fawn?" she asked hopefully.

"Deer do use this trail, but I doubt if we'll spot any. If you look out the window near dusk you'll probably see some feeding."

A chickadee, invisible in the pines, called from overhead. Sunlight shafted through the branches in slanting columns of gold. Recalling the awe she'd felt as a child in these Catskill woods, Alida realized she had the same breathless sense of wonder now and stopped to savor the glory surrounding her.

Justin looked back. "Tired?"

She shook her head, waving her hand to take in all she could see and hear. "It's so lovely and peaceful under the trees."

"I've always liked the woods." He waited for her to catch up with him. "No other place is like the Catskills."

"Are there still wildcats in these mountains?"

"You hear one caterwauling once in awhile at night. I haven't seen a wildcat since I was a kid, and that one was dead, shot by the groundsman."

"There were lots of them in the early days, I've heard. Isn't that what 'Catskills' means?"

"There are two schools of thought. Some claim the mountains were called after a stream not too far away from here—Cats Kill. Kill is Dutch for stream. And they say the stream was named after Jacob Cats, an early Dutch poet. Their argument is that Dutch plurals are made by adding 'e' or 'en' to a word. The plural of katt—Dutch for cat—is katten or katte, not katts. So they feel it's obvious the mountains weren't named for the wildcats that haunted them but for Jacob Cats. I'll give you an example of his work: 'Nineteen nay-says o' a maiden are ha'f a grant.' Like it?"

Alida grimaced. "Do you really believe the mountains were named after him?"

"I don't think it matters. How about you?"

"I prefer to think the mountains were named for the wildcats the early settlers found. Better still, I like the Indian name—Onti Ora, Mountains of the Sky."

"You're obviously a romantic."

Alida raised an eyebrow. "Actually I'm quite practical."

"You expect me to believe a woman who insists on staying by herself in a decaying old house on an isolated mountain is practical?"

Alida was about to explain her childhood attraction to the McLeod mansion when they came to a clearing.

"This used to be the road to the Randolph place," Justin said. "It's so overgrown now you couldn't even get up it with a four-wheel drive."

Walking side by side, they followed the one-time road, Alida all too aware of Justin's disturbing nearness. Around a sharp curve she saw a fence, once white but now gray, wandering in a half-circle in and out of the undergrowth.

"The house was there." Justin pointed. "We'll walk over."

Alida noticed a black metal post with a ring through the top poking above a cluster of laurel. Beside the post was a large stone. She frowned, wondering what the purpose of post and stone could have been and then realized it must be a hitching post. In the old days the stone was used to climb into a carriage or mount a horse.

A depression showed where the cellar of the Randolph house had been and an uneven line of mortared stones traced the outline of the house.

The McLeod mansion won't have even this much left, she thought unhappily. Looking away from the ruins, she noticed the remnants of what must have been a small apple orchard.

Justin followed her gaze. "I tried the apples last fall. They're wormy."

"If I did happen to be a romantic," she said tartly, "you certainly would cure me in no time."

He grinned at her.

"Does this belong to your father now?" she asked, although she was almost positive of the answer. David McLeod owned this entire side of the mountain.

"Yes. My grandfather bought the land from Colonel Randolph's widow a few years after the fire."

"The Randolphs are gone from the area then?"

"No, Margaret's still living in Persis. She never married."

Had Stuart McLeod's disappearance turned Margaret Randolph against men? Alida wondered. She glanced at Justin. The sun highlighted his hair, gilding it an even richer gold. The exertion of the walk made his T-shirt cling damply to his powerful torso, and his jeans fit almost too well. Had *he* ever married, was a wife waiting for him in California?

"What did Stuart look like?" she asked abruptly, wanting to return from the danger of the here and now to the safety of the past.

"I've been told I resemble him," Justin said.

She nodded. No wonder Margaret had never forgotten Stuart. Every atom of her being was aware of Justin. She longed to have him touch her and at the same time feared her own reaction if he did. It would be all too easy for her to fall into his arms. Merely thinking about him holding her made her heart flutter. What was the matter with her?

Alida turned abruptly from the ruins of the Randolph house and started back the way they'd come. Justin caught up with her a moment later.

"We'll go back by a different route," he said.

They followed the remnants of the Randolphs' private road downhill, stopping along the way to pick and eat blackcaps from the prickly canes of wild raspberries. The berries' tart sweetness lingered on her tongue. At last they came out on the main road. A few minutes later she saw the tower of the gatehouse above the trees and stopped, looking back, trying to picture where the Randolph house had been in relation to the McLeod mansion.

As if reading her mind he said, "Colonel Randolph's place sat on a knoll a little above our house, about a mile away through the woods."

She nodded, thinking that later she'd ask him to locate the ruins for her on her map of the McLeod property.

Near the gatehouse, Mrs. Danford was bent over her roses, cutting off faded blooms. She straightened when Justin greeted her, her black eyes flicking over Alida before fastening on Justin. She gave him the ghost of a smile, snipped off a dark red rose with the sharp secateurs she carried and limped toward them.

"Good morning, Mrs. Danford," Alida said.

The old woman ignored her, handing Justin the rose. Once again she wore an outdated black dress, the hem straggling unevenly, and dark stockings with heavy black shoes.

"Have you met Ms. Drury?" Justin asked her.

"She's staying up at the house." Mrs. Danford's voice was rusty and harsh with no trace of the regional accent. "No good will come of it."

Justin treated the comment as a joke. "I've told her the same thing, but she's a stubborn one."

"It's dangerous," Mrs. Danford persisted. "The house is best left empty until they tear it down."

Alida stared at the woman's wrinkled face, tanned a deep brown from the sun. What on earth was she talking about?

"You don't believe me," Mrs. Danford said to Alida. "You don't think I can feel what can't be seen. There's a residue left in that house, something there seeks to live again. Leave while you still are able to go."

She means ghosts, Alida told herself. The old woman fancies she's psychic. Well, I don't believe in ghosts. All the same, a chill crept along her spine as she gazed into Mrs. Danford's penetrating black eyes.

"Thanks for the rose." Justin touched Mrs. Danford on the shoulder but said nothing at all about her strange comments. He merely took Alida's hand and urged her past the gatehouse and up the drive toward the mansion.

"What's the matter with her?" Alida asked when they were out of hearing.

"She's harmless. Living like a hermit makes her a bit odd."

"Who is she?"

Justin shrugged. "My father befriended her a few years back. I really don't know much about her. If she lived in New York City I suppose she might become a bag lady."

"Does she act as caretaker to the mansion at all?"

"No. She has no keys to the house, she has nothing to do with it." He held out the rose to Alida, offering it to her.

She shook her head. "I prefer your brown-eyed susans."

In truth she did like roses but somehow she didn't want the one Mrs. Danford had given to Justin.

He reached up and laid the rose in the vee of a maple branch, saying, "This is the shortcut; now it's marked for you."

Alida followed him off the drive into the trees and as the branches closed overhead she felt a sense of both relief and anticipation. Mrs. Danford, and everything else, was shut out. There were only the two of them in the pine-scented green of the woods.

He showed her the remains of a tree house in an ancient maple, led her on to where a pond glimmered in the sun filtering through the branches. Suddenly Alida remembered being here before.

She'd been ten and secretly trailing the big boys, Justin and his friends, slipping from one tree to the next behind them, pretending she was an Indian tracking intruders on her tribal ground. Mostly, though, she just wanted to be near Justin, even though her mother had warned her not to bother him. She never tired of watching him.

"You used to pole a raft on this pond," Alida told Justin. "You, a red-headed boy and one with freckles."

He stopped and stared at her, puzzlement in his eyes.

"There was a mast on the raft where you flew a pirate's skull and crossbones."

Justin shouted with laughter. "Got it!" he cried. "You were the dark-haired imp who shadowed me all one summer—I'd all but forgotten. It was the last summer I spent here, the last any of us spent here."

"I remember that summer very well. It's why I wanted to stay in the mansion one last time. I guess I really did plague you and your friends."

"I couldn't turn around without finding you behind me. You were relentless. I half expected to find you under my bed at night."

Alida flushed, hoping he'd never know how she'd once crept into his room when he was gone and behaved like Goldilocks, sitting in his chair, lying on his bed, touching what he'd touched, all the time afraid one of the servants would catch her.

It was that ten-year-old Alida she had to watch out for now; the girl with the childish crush on Justin lived within her yet. What else made her pulses pound and her breath catch at his look, at his smile?

Justin took two steps, closing the gap between them. He used his forefinger to tip up her chin so she had to meet his gaze. His smile faded as their eyes met. "I felt somehow that I knew you from the moment I saw you yesterday," he said huskily.

"I...I knew you right away," she managed to say. Ripples of excitement fanned through her as his hands touched her shoulders and slid caressingly down her arms.

"You should have told me."

"I didn't think you'd remember me."

"Even then you were memorable. Now..." His words trailed off as he bent his head.

His lips touched hers lightly, drifting over her mouth in delicate exploration. The tip of his tongue traced the outline of her lips, taking her breath away.

"Mmmm," he murmured. "You taste like raspberries."

Pulling her closer, his kiss deepened, seeking a response she couldn't deny. Alida's arms slipped around his neck, holding him to her as her lips answered his, the warmth of his mouth setting her ablaze with the need for more. She was no longer a child. She'd grown into a woman and what she felt had nothing to do with being ten years old.

Rightly or wrongly, she wanted Justin as a woman wants a man, and she was helpless to conceal her yearning.

Four

Justin's kiss stayed with Alida for the rest of the day. Though she'd ended the embrace abruptly, fearful of the consequences, she couldn't rid herself of the emotions his touch had evoked. Justin left soon afterward, with no indication of when or if they'd meet again.

It would be best if they didn't, but that might be difficult. She still had business to take care of with his father. She'd have to try to avoid being alone with Justin. If he kissed her again she wasn't sure she'd be able to pull away.

During the afternoon, Alida drove into Persis, stocked up on groceries and bought a battery-powered lantern. As she headed back to her car, thunder rumbled in the distance. By the time she was on the highway toward Thunder King, the day had darkened, gray clouds covering the sun. She saw a jagged streak of lightning over the mountain, but the roll of thunder followed so much later she realized the storm was farther away then it looked.

Sure enough, by the time she reached the mansion the sun shone again and the afternoon was even more oppressively hot and humid. Alida, drenched with perspiration after she'd finished unloading the car, carried a chair onto the shaded side porch to sit and cool off.

A brilliant green hummingbird, ruby flashing like a gem at his throat, probed the depths of a pink rose of sharon flower, his tiny wings a blur of speed. Birds and flowers, she thought. Beauty. Peacefulness.

A second hummingbird darted toward the bush and the first ceased his nectar hunting, turning on the newcomer with an indignant chirr-r-r, fiercely defending his territory by aggressive rushes until the second bird finally gave up and retreated.

So much for peace.

The katydids' monotonous three-syllable call provided a background for the trills and cheeps of unseen birds foraging in the trees and bushes. Alida's attention focused on a plaintive far-off cry as she tried to decide what was making the noise. It sounded like a cat, no, more like a kitten. She stood up.

"Kitty, kitty?" she called.

No cat appeared and after a moment she sank back down onto the chair. It could be a mockingbird—they imitated everything they heard.

She must remember to watch for deer this evening. Justin had said all she had to do was look out a window. Justin...

What had he felt when he kissed her? Desire for a woman, any woman? Or was she as special to him as he was to her? Alida shook her head, telling herself it made no difference since there'd be no encore.

Later, as she ate a light supper, she couldn't help thinking about their being together at breakfast. He'd sat across from her at the table, the brown-eyed susans their centerpiece, with those amber eyes that warmed her heart intent on hers. Now the wildflowers drooped. Strong and sturdy while growing outdoors, they didn't last once picked.

Touching the limp golden petals, she wondered if the brown-eyed susans were a symbol. She'd chosen them over a rose and roses in a vase stayed fresh for a long time.

At dusk thunder rumbled again, but by the time she went to bed no rain had fallen. A nearly full moon rode the sky, its pale light transforming the grounds into a wonderland of silver-tinged beauty. In fascination she watched a doe and her fawn walk with quiet grace from the trees to feed on the grass, then smiled to see a family of skunks arrive to dig for grubs in the lawn, all but standing on their heads in their search.

Once in bed Alida fell asleep quickly.

It was dark. Night. She stood grasping a railing, staring at a red glare above the trees. Yet though she saw the glare and smelled the acrid scent of smoke drifting on the night breeze, somehow she didn't seem to be herself. It wasn't Alida Drury who stood on the balcony.

She tightened her hold on the railing, fearing the fire was out of control and worrying that the woods might catch if the wind blew embers from the burning house into the trees. It was a house that burned, she knew, for she'd been there when the fire started and had seen the small glow grow and spread. Now flames engulfed the house and sent fiery scouts through the woods seeking new fuel, seeking her . . .

Alida sat up in bed, her heart hammering in her chest. The pungent stench of something burning filled her nostrils. A dream, she thought confusedly, yet the smell didn't dissipate. She jumped up and flicked on the overhead light, blinking in the glare. Nothing was burning in the bedroom.

Where?

She searched the apartment without finding any fire, grabbed up her lantern and was about to unbolt the door to the foyer when she decided the smell had been strongest in the kitchen. Returning, she confirmed her suspicion and unbolted the door to the side porch. Smoke coiled about her, pouring into the kitchen.

Alida grabbed the basin she'd used for a dishpan and quickly filled it with water. Coughing, she sluiced the water toward what seemed to be the source of the smoke—something burning in the corner of the porch near her door. Four more basins of water quenched the smoldering fire. With the handle of a broom, she pushed the sodden, blackened mass of cloth down the steps onto the rock walkway, then tossed more water onto it.

By the light of her lantern, she examined the floor of the porch and the siding of the house where the rags had been burning, running her hands over the wood to be certain no spark escaped her. She rechecked the charred rags on the walk below. The fire was out.

Suddenly she felt vulnerable, alone here, barefoot and in her nightgown, standing in a circle of light from

her lantern with darkness surrounding her. Did unseen eyes watch her? Fear flickered in her mind, wisps
of uneasy speculation.

How had the fire started?

As she retreated up the steps, Alida tried to recall if
there'd been a bundle of rags in that corner when she'd
sat on the porch earlier. She was almost certain there
hadn't been. But that meant human hands had placed
them there, had ignited the fire.

Why?

Safely inside the kitchen, she rebolted the door. If
the fire was deliberately set, had the intent been to
burn down the mansion? She shook her head. It would
have been a long time before the flames would have
spread enough to be dangerous.

Her car under the porte cochere proclaimed the fact
she was staying in the apartment. If someone had
wanted to burn the house down, they'd have chosen a
spot as far away from her quarters as possible so she
wouldn't immediately smell the smoke. They'd have
set a more efficient blaze, maybe used gasoline.

Certainly whoever it was must have known she'd
discover the rags before much damage was done. Had
the rags been set afire to frighten her into leaving the
mansion? Despite the warm night, Alida shivered at
the thought.

Who didn't want her here? Some faceless searcher
after the diamond brooch who wanted the mansion
left vacant? Or someone whose face she knew? Mrs.
Danford had said no good would come of her being
here, but she couldn't visualize the old woman limp-
ing up that long hill from the gatehouse in the middle
of the night to set the fire.

The only other person she knew who might not want her here was Justin.

Slowly she walked into the bedroom hugging herself against her inner chill. In bed, she bunched the pillows behind her and sat up with the overhead light on. In fact, every light in the apartment was lit. Only when the chirp of birds announced the dawn did Alida slide down in bed, close her eyes and sleep.

Her appointment with David McLeod was for two in the afternoon, so Alida hadn't set her alarm. She awoke at noon. After showering she pulled on jeans and a T-shirt and hurried onto the side porch. No, it hadn't been a bad dream. The blackened rags on the walk stank of damp ashes. She shoved them into a plastic bag and carried it to a trash barrel near the storage shed.

As she breakfasted on coffee and toast, last night's fire and her fears seemed less menacing, despite the evidence she'd just disposed of. With the hot, bright sun heating the day, she felt she'd been more intimidated than necessary.

In the predawn hours she'd planned to pack and find a motel as soon as possible, but now she decided to wait until after her meeting with David. After dressing for the appointment, she paused to check her appearance in the mirror attached to the inside of the bedroom door.

Her black hair, freshly washed and blow-dried, fell in soft, natural waves to her shoulders, her apricot lip gloss matched the vee-neck cotton knit shell she wore with her cream silk suit skirt—it was much too hot to put on the jacket. Cream colored pumps with a compromise heel—not too high as to be frivolous, not so low as to be unflattering—completed the outfit. Alida nodded. Attractively businesslike.

To her surprise David McLeod answered the door himself. "I thought we'd sit on the patio," he told her.

He led the way to the back of the lodge. In the space between the two wings, water shimmered in a swimming pool set in the center of a vast brick patio with chairs and tables scattered around it. The top and sides of the entire area were screened.

David noticed her glancing at the redwood-framed screening. "That's one problem with eastern summers," he said. "The bugs enjoy the warm weather as much as we do. My host seems to have outwitted them."

It was pleasant by the pool with tall pines shading them from the relentless July sun.

"Every so often it clouds up and thunders," she said. "I keep expecting rain but then the sun comes back."

David smiled. "That's how Thunder King got its name. Eventually the storm will break, though it may take awhile. How are you getting along in the apartment?"

Alida's polite smile faded. "I put out a fire on the porch last night. A pile of rags smoldering. No damage was done but—"

"Damn those backpackers!" David leaned forward in his chair. "If you only knew the trouble I've had with trespassers, mostly those on foot. It'll be a relief to transfer the problem to Kentin Hotels."

"I'm not sure the fire was caused by a hiker."

"It was, I'm sure of it. They toss lit cigarettes anywhere without thinking of the consequences. Three years ago it took three volunteer fire companies to put out a brush fire lower down the mountain started by an irresponsible backpacker.''

Alida hesitated. Was it possible David was right? The rags hadn't been there earlier, but suppose a hiker had sat on the porch to rest and smoke, discarding dirty garments he no longer wanted, carelessly flipping a cigarette butt away afterward. Certainly it could have happened that way.

"Finding the fire and having to put it out must have upset you," David went on. "I'll understand if you move out and I'll be glad to pay for your motel room."

"KHI covers my stay in the Catskills. Thanks for your offer, but I think I'll stick it out where I am." Alida heard her words with amazement. She hadn't known she was going to say such a thing until she'd said it.

"Are you certain? I wouldn't blame you if—"

"Mr. McLeod, I'm not a quitter. The fire did no damage to the house nor did it harm me. Very likely it was accidental, as you said."

Do I really mean this? Alida asked herself. How will I feel when it gets dark? She sat a bit straighter. What she'd told him about not being a quitter was true. Alida Drury finished what she started.

David's sudden grin lighted his face so he looked years younger, and for the first time she noted some resemblance to Justin. "I like your spirit. I'm sorry about the day before yesterday, I didn't mean to unsettle you."

"It was my fault for arriving unannounced."

"You really don't remind me of Priscilla at all. It's the effect coming back here has on me, especially at this time of the year."

"Justin told me a little about Priscilla."

David's eyes looked past her, unfocused, as though looking into the past. "I remember the December day she came and my father drove her up to the house from the train station. Stuart and I stood shivering on his balcony hoping to get a glimpse before we had to go downstairs and meet her. At least *I* was hoping to see her. Stuart was probably humoring me. He was the best-natured person in the world, he couldn't be unkind to anyone. Of course that got him into a few scrapes; you have to learn to say no once in awhile.

"'She looks like a gypsy,' Stuart whispered to me when Priscilla got out of father's big black Buick. I thought she looked like a child because she was so small, smaller than I was, even though she was fifteen and I wasn't quite thirteen. I hoped we'd be friends, she'd be my sister and I'd do my best to be her brother."

"What was she like?"

David didn't answer for so long Alida began to be afraid he was annoyed at her question.

"I don't really know," he said at last. "Priscilla was one of those people who seem to be acting all the time. Pretending. Just when I thought I was getting to know her she'd change and be someone else. Stuart didn't notice, but I did. He liked her and I didn't. Though I tried very hard to, especially after my parents adopted her and she really became my sister.

"I felt terribly guilty. Here was this homeless orphan. But she was spiteful. And she told lies. She had to have her own way, no matter who got hurt. I still believe that if Priscilla had never come into the house, everything would have been all right. Stuart wouldn't have left, Margaret wouldn't have wasted her life, even Justin would be different."

"Justin?" Alida's voice reflected her surprise.

"Justin's a fine son, I don't mean to imply he isn't. But he's restless. Like Stuart. Brilliant and restless. Never settles anywhere. A year here, two years there. Now he spends half his time under the sea in California. I blame it on myself. Priscilla affected us all, you see, and I never got over it, never was a proper father to Justin."

Alida, rather overwhelmed by these confidences from David McLeod, didn't know what to say. "Justin spends his time under the sea?" she finally managed.

David sighed. "He's an oceanographer. Nothing wrong with that, I suppose." He looked directly at Alida. "I keep hoping he'll settle down. Marry. Have children. Maybe I can enjoy my grandchildren as I never could enjoy my son. I don't mean to embarrass you by rattling on about my life. Somehow, though, it seems as though I've known you for a long time."

Because I reminded him of Priscilla at first, she thought. She found herself warming to David McLeod. He seemed to her to be lonely and unhappy. Yet he wasn't an old man, he had time to enjoy life if only he would. And in her heart she rejoiced at the discovery that Justin wasn't married.

Knowles appeared with a tray of drinks and Alida gratefully accepted a tall lemonade, as did David. When Knowles had gone, David settled back in his chair.

"Well, down to business. I know Kentin Hotels must have thought it strange when I asked for a face-to-face meeting before I signed the final papers. The truth is I'm eccentric and I make no bones about it. I always insist on seeing a representative of those I do business with. I'm glad they sent you—you seem to be a competent and feisty young woman. Pretty besides. You can assure your employers I'll hold to my end of the agreement, and the necessary documents will be in their hands as soon as my lawyers get through the fine print."

Alida, who'd reached for her portfolio when David mentioned business, held it unopened in her lap. "Don't you want me to show you any of the plans?"

"No. I've seen and heard all I need to know. Both Kentin Hotels and I are satisfied with the deal we've made, and that's all that matters. I should have gotten rid of the place years ago."

"If you're certain you don't want to see any of the material I've brought, then I won't impose on your time," she said, setting down the case and starting to rise. "I appreciate—"

He waved her back into the chair. "Don't rush off, finish your lemonade. I enjoy your company. In fact, if you don't have a deadline to get back to Phoenix, why not stay on at the apartment for a few more days? Wait until the lawyers are satisfied. Who knows, they may balk at a comma or a semicolon." He smiled at her.

"You're very kind." She didn't want to refuse outright. Besides, David could be right about the lawyers. It might be best to stay on until the actual signing to be sure nothing went wrong.

Be honest, she chided herself, the reason you don't want to leave the Catskills is Justin. Ruefully she admitted that he was certainly part of the reason. A big part.

"Justin didn't want me to sell the place, you know. He fought the sale to Kentin Hotels."

David's words jarred her.

"He reminds me of Stuart in many ways. True, Justin learned to say no with great vehemence at an early age, but otherwise..." His words trailed off and again he looked into his own mind rather than at her.

Alida sipped her lemonade and waited.

"I hate the old house," he said at last, his voice choked as though he held back tears. "My memories of it are all bad, and I've never set foot on the property since the day we moved. I never will again. Tear it down, build a resort in its place. Wipe the McLeod mansion and its ill fortune from the face of the earth."

As Alida drove into Persis after her visit with David, she thought not of him or of Justin but of Priscilla. An orphan forced by war from her own country, arriving in an alien land to live with strangers, Priscilla must have been frightened and lonely. She couldn't have felt at home with her new parents, and must rather have felt she didn't belong anywhere.

I've never really belonged anywhere, either, Alida told herself. Poor Priscilla. Perhaps she'd merely been a catalyst in what had happened—she'd been no more than sixteen, after all.

When Alida finished shopping it was after five. Since she'd bought no perishables she decided to stay and have dinner in the village. The Ferns appeared to be the best choice of the several restaurants and diners. The dining room, she found, was below street level, with a gift shop on the main floor.

"Table for two?" the host asked, looking behind her as if expecting a man to materialize out of thin air.

"For one," she said somewhat tartly. Didn't women ever dine alone in Persis?

She refused to sit next to the swinging door to the kitchen, asking politely but firmly for one of the small tables overlooking the fernery at the far end of the room. The waitress who took her order was bright and friendly and did much to alleviate Alida's first, unfavorable impression of The Ferns.

"I'd have the flounder if I was you," the waitress said when Alida asked her to recommend an entree. "It came in fresh today and the chef broils it real nice. Don't take the rice, though, the baked potatoes are usually better."

While she sipped a glass of Chablis, waiting for her meal, Alida couldn't help notice that the others in the uncrowded dining room, all men-women couples, were eyeing her surreptitiously. She found herself tensing and tried to relax. Although she didn't often eat out alone, she had certainly done so in the past and it never bothered her.

It must be this small town. Everyone seemed to watch what everyone else did—especially if you were a stranger. The flounder was good, melting in her mouth. Alida made up her mind to leave her waitress a larger tip than necessary. As she ate, the room filled rapidly; evidently people in the area were early diners. By the time she finished her meal only the table next to hers, with a reserved card prominently displayed, was empty.

Sitting with her coffee, she heard a stir run through the dining room and, curious, looked around. An attractive blonde wearing a violet sundress with a low vee neck stood at the entrance.

"So she's still chasing him after all these years," the woman at the table for four behind her said.

"I saw her yesterday in Newman's and by the size of that diamond on her fourth finger, I think she's caught him," another woman responded.

The words seemed to pierce Alida's heart. At that moment Justin McLeod appeared beside the blonde, who smiled up at him as she took his arm. For a moment Alida contemplated rising and hurrying from the room but quelled the impulse.

Justin was nothing to her; why should she be upset?

A hard knot gathered in her stomach as she watched the host lead Justin and the blonde toward the empty table next to hers. She couldn't stop her eyes from flicking to the woman's left hand, to the diamond solitaire on her ring finger.

"Alida!" Justin sounded surprised.

She raised her chin and met his glance. "Hello, Justin."

"Renée, this is Alida Drury of Kentin Hotels," he said. "Alida, Renée Shroeder."

Renée smiled coolly, Alida murmured a greeting.

"Oh, you've already eaten," Justin said. "Won't you join us for an after-dinner drink?"

Join them! "Thank you, no," Alida managed to say.

Justin looked as though he intended to go on talking to her, but Renée put her hand on his arm. "Darling, I'm starved." Her voice was low and intimate.

As Justin turned to seat Renée at their table, Alida rose and strode toward the stairs, feeling that every eye in the room was on her. The entire group of diners were busy speculating who the strange dark woman might be and what it might mean that Justin McLeod apparently knew her.

I'll stay at the mansion tonight, she told herself as her car climbed the mountain. Tomorrow I'll make my return reservation to Phoenix. David assured me the deal is solid; I don't need to remain here.

As for Justin, like so many other men, he's merely an opportunist where women are concerned. Just because he's engaged to one doesn't mean he won't kiss another. You're well rid of him, lucky you didn't have time to make a complete fool of yourself.

The trouble was, her head knew this was true, but her heart ached with yearning. Her lips remembered Justin's kiss, her body longed to be held against his again. No matter what.

Five

Moonlight lay like a gauze curtain over the trees, and glowed from the grass and shrubs. The world seemed a fairyland where dreams came true, dreams of love and adventure and happiness.

Alida pictured the mansion as it had once been, proud and beautiful. In a hostess gown of silk brocade, she stood in the foyer beneath the gleaming chandelier welcoming dinner guests in long gowns and dinner jackets, while beside her stood the man of the house—Justin.

Over the heads of those he greeted, he smiled at her, his eyes promising untold pleasures to come later, when the guests were gone. Pleasures only the two of them would share....

Movement near the woods caught her eye and the fantasy faded as she waited for the doe and her fawn to appear again. Instead, a buck with many-pronged antlers stepped onto the lawn, looked around, then suddenly turned and leaped back into the trees. Alida had neither seen nor heard anything that might have startled him, and the katydids and frogs chorused on, undisturbed.

Dreams didn't come true, you'd think she'd have learned that by now. Justin had entered her life as briefly as the deer she'd just seen.

Alida drew the shade down, undressed and got ready for bed. She plugged the recently bought night-light into a socket near the door and turned out all the other lights. For awhile she lay in bed stiff with tension, but when her eyes grew used to the darkness and she saw that in the glow of the night-light she could make out the objects in the room, she began to relax. The only harm that would come to her here, she assured herself, was to her emotions, and that was as much her fault as anyone else's.

Had Justin promised her undying love, had he mentioned a commitment of any kind? Of course not. Any commitment had been on her part. She shifted restlessly, thinking of how she'd invited his caresses by making it obvious to him how attracted she was.

Is that how it had been when Priscilla came here? she wondered. If Stuart had been as good-looking as Justin, Priscilla must have lost her heart to him. Perhaps he hadn't been able to resist her adoration despite her youth and the fact that he was supposed to be engaged to Margaret Randolph.

Alida turned onto her side. There was no point in going over what had happened long ago. Tomorrow she'd be leaving the Catskills, and in a month she'd have forgotten Priscilla's name.

And Justin's name as well? Would she ever forget Justin?

She gritted her teeth and flipped onto her back. Deliberately she began the relaxation techniques she'd learned in her yoga class, pushing all thoughts from her mind.

Alida woke abruptly, a screech ringing in her ears. She flew out of bed, listening. From close by a cat yowled defiantly. Grabbing the lantern, she hurried to the kitchen door, unbolted it and stepped onto the porch.

Near the foot of the steps a dark shape rose into the air, wings flapping, startling her. An owl, she told herself.

"Kitty?" she called tentatively.

A plaintive mew answered, but no cat appeared.

Alida shone the light onto the bushes, saw the gleam of eyes underneath the lowest branches. She descended the steps and crouched, holding out her hand. "I won't hurt you," she crooned. "Come to me, kitty." Over and over she murmured soothingly but couldn't coax the cat from its hiding place.

At last she went inside and filled a small bowl with milk, placing it near the bush while she sat on the steps and waited. The cat crept to the bowl, lowered its head and lapped hungrily at the milk. It was black and white, a skinny, bedraggled half-grown kitten.

By inching toward the animal, Alida managed to reach it before the cat took alarm and, with one finger, she stroked the tiny head. By the time it finished the milk its fear of her was gone and she carried it into the house.

In the bright light of the kitchen, she saw the cat was a female with a shallow gash along her left flank. The owl had been hunting the cat, Alida thought, and almost captured her. One of its talons must have raked the cat's side.

She filled a basin with warm water and washed the cat thoroughly, murmuring, "Poor little thing, you were lucky to escape that owl. And you're half-starved, I'll have to fatten you up. What would have happened to you if I hadn't been here tonight? I almost wasn't, you know—you *are* lucky."

By the time she sat drying the purring cat in her lap, she'd decided to name it Lady Luck.

"Once you're good and dry you can sleep with me. We'll . . ." Her words trailed off as her head came up, listening.

A motor growled outside, brakes squealed, a car door slammed. Alida rose, clutching the towel-wrapped cat to her breast. Feet clattered up the side porch steps and a fist banged on the door.

"Damn it, Alida, let me in!"

She stared unbelievingly. "Justin?"

"Yes. Let me in."

Alida unbolted the door.

Justin flung it open and strode into the kitchen. "What in hell are you doing here?"

She gathered her wits. "I'm drying my new cat. I just gave her a bath. More to the point, what are you doing here?"

"I came up to talk some sense into you. Why would you want to stay in this place after someone set that fire last night? My father told me what happened, and I told him he should never have let you come back here. What's the matter with you?"

Alida glared at him. "Nothing's the matter with me. The fire was minor, I wasn't hurt. Why shouldn't I stay in the apartment?"

"This place is a firetrap. You shouldn't be here, no one should. Why are you so stubborn?"

The cat squirmed in Alida's grasp, protesting, and she realized her grip on it had tightened. She put the towel and cat down on a chair; then, suddenly aware of her thin and revealing nightgown, edged toward the bedroom.

Justin closed the gap between them, taking her by the shoulders. "You make me so damn mad," he growled, shaking her.

Before she could wrench away, she saw his eyes change, saw the anger replaced by desire. His hands slid down her arms to pull her to him, igniting her own smoldering need.

His mouth crushed hers, she felt the hard length of his body against her breasts, her thighs, searing through the thin cotton of her gown. She had no control over her flare of response. Her arms held him, her lips answered his.

His tongue sought hers, thrusting between her lips so she tasted the full flavor of his mouth—piquant and stimulating. He smelled of pine, of the July night and of himself, the most erotic odor of all.

When his fingers traced the curve of her breast, sparks of excitement flared deep within her. She wanted to feel his touch everywhere, wanted this delicious whirling kaleidoscope of sensation to go on forever.

His lips at her ear murmured her name, his warm breath sending thrilling waves along her nerve endings. How soft the hair at his nape was, how silky under her fingers.

Renée.

The two syllables echoed in her mind, reverberating throughout her body. Renée was his choice, the woman he meant to marry. What did that make her—second best?

Alida brought her hands between them, pushing against Justin's chest. His eyes were dark with passion as he raised his head to look down at her.

"I don't want..." she began, speaking with effort, "please don't...oh, why don't you leave me alone?"

He drew back and his arms dropped away from her. She crossed her own arms over her breasts, hugging herself.

"Please go," she whispered.

"If that's what you want." He eyed her consideringly. "Somehow I don't think it is."

Alida snatched up the cat, holding it between them, hardly noticing its claws digging into her shoulder. "Goodnight, Justin," she said as coolly as she could.

He shrugged and turned to the door. "I won't be far away. Call if you need me."

Alida shot the bolt behind him and carried the cat into her bedroom. Need him? She'd never felt this way about a man before, never experienced such an aching need. Yet she wouldn't allow herself to give way. Alida Drury was no man's second choice.

The cat woke Alida in the morning by licking her face. After she'd let Lady outside, she showered and dressed, putting on pale yellow shorts with a sleeveless top of white and yellow stripes.

I can't stay in the Catskills any longer, she told herself as she brushed her hair. This wild, crazy desire for Justin is bound to bring trouble if I don't leave right away.

Just thinking about him brought back the hungry excitement she'd felt in his arms last night. She watched her mirror image's eyes brighten, her cheeks turn pink, and she threw down the brush, turning away.

Once she and the cat finished their breakfast, she'd begin to pack. But when she went to the door to call Lady, a fiftyish woman was standing on the porch, hand raised to knock.

"I'm Margaret Randolph," she said. "I heard someone was staying here and since there's no phone I dropped by to ask you if you'd like to have lunch with me later this week."

Alida introduced herself, adding, "Won't you come in?"

"For just a minute or two. I haven't been in this house for more years than I care to remember."

"It's kind of you to invite me to lunch, but I don't think I'll be staying here that long. I'm here for Kentin Hotels. Perhaps you've heard we're buying the estate."

"Oh, yes." Margaret looked around the kitchen with an abstracted air. "They've changed things."

Alida eyed the graying woman. She must be older than David if she was Stuart's age, but she looked younger. Her face was relatively unlined, her figure still neatly attractive. Lady, who'd darted inside when Margaret, came in, brushed against Alida's ankles, mewing.

"Don't let me keep you from feeding your cat," Margaret said.

Alida took a can of white meat tuna she'd bought for herself from the cupboard and opened it. Lady ate as though she'd never get another meal.

"I'm about to make coffee, won't you have some?" Alida asked.

Margaret shook her head, yet made no move to leave. "It should have burned down, too," she said suddenly. "This house should have burned the same night my father's did. I wish it had."

Alida stared at her.

Margaret flushed. "I'm sorry. You must think I'm crazy. I don't know what possessed me to say that, even though it's truly the way I feel. Certainly my past is of no concern to you, and I have no business forcing it on you. Being in this house again brought on that outburst. Please forgive me."

"You haven't upset me," Alida assured her.

"I must go, yet I'd like to talk to you. Not here, not in this house. How about tomorrow, would you be able to have lunch with me then?"

Alida hesitated. It's possible she wouldn't be able to arrange for a flight today, and she was curious about Margaret. "I'm not sure. If I'm still here, I'd like to."

"What I'll do is have lunch at The Ferns myself tomorrow. If you can join me about twelve-thirty I'd love to have you."

"If I can make it, I will."

Margaret's smile transformed her face, making the pretty girl she once had been come alive for a moment. "I'll hope to see you. I'm really not the mad woman of Persis as a rule."

After Margaret left, Alida ate her toast and coffee. On the whole, she'd rather liked Margaret Randolph, but the mention of the fire had shaken her. Was it possible Margaret could be responsible for the rag fire? And why did she want to talk to Alida?

Lady was nowhere in sight. Alida, who'd already decided to take the cat back to Phoenix with her, called and called, then searched the apartment without finding the cat. Perhaps Lady had slipped outside when Margaret left. She opened the door and called again. Lady didn't come.

Alida left the porch and searched among the bushes. No cat. She circled the house, calling, but Lady didn't appear. Alida looked toward the trees. Was it possible the cat had gone into the woods? She ought to be packing, getting ready to drive into Persis to call the airline for a return flight, but first she wanted to find Lady. She headed for the woods behind the house.

Once among the trees, Alida tried to locate the path Justin had showed her yesterday, but could not. "Kitty?" she called. "Where are you, Lady Luck?"

"Won't I do?" Justin's voice asked.

She swung around. He lounged under a pine where he'd staked a small green tent and set up a camp stove.

"What are you doing here?" she demanded.

"My home away from home," he told her. "If you insist on being stubborn, someone has to watch over you at night."

Now was the time to raise an eyebrow and inform him he'd gone to a great deal of trouble for nothing. She was leaving in a few hours and he'd never be inconvenienced by her stubbornness again. Alida willed herself to say the words but all she could seem to do was gaze at Justin in his cutoffs and sandals.

Curls of crisp golden hair matted his broad chest and veed downward. He stood with legs slightly apart, muscled thighs disappearing into the ragged edges of the denim cutoffs that rode low on his slim hips.

"I think I prefer the blue nightgown," he said, "but I like you in shorts, too."

She flushed, angry at herself. Where was the cool, poised woman who'd defanged the office wolf at KHI? She'd never been easily flustered, but Justin could reduce her to incoherence in nothing flat.

"I'm looking for my cat," she said crisply. "Have you seen her?"

He shook his head. "Come and see my tent," he invited.

"I haven't time. I must find Lady because I—"

"I'll help you if it's that important. Did you see her go into the woods?"

"No, but she isn't around the house. Really, you don't need to..." Her words trailed away as he strode to her and stood inches away, looking down at her.

"Why are you so afraid of me?" he asked softly.

"I—I'm not afraid." She knew the pulse in her neck was throbbing madly and hoped he wouldn't notice. Her breath caught in her throat as his fingertips trailed along her cheek.

"You're very lovely, Alida. I want you and you know it. What you won't admit is that you want me. I see it in your eyes, feel it when you respond to me. Why do you hold back?"

"I'm here on business." Her words sounded stilted in her own ears.

"Business that's been settled, so my father says."

The small space between them vibrated with his virile magnetism. He was so close she could feel the heat of his body. Powerless to move away, she stared into his amber eyes and lost herself in their glowing, golden depths.

No! she admonished herself. No!

With a great effort of will, Alida sidestepped, trying to put distance between them. He followed her. Searching for anything to break the spell he'd cast over her, all she could find to say was, "Margaret Randolph visited me this morning. Do you think she could have set the fire?"

Her words stopped Justin's advance. He frowned, shaking his head. "Not Margaret. Why would she?"

"She told me she wished the McLeod mansion had burned the night the Randolph place did. Maybe she's trying to carry out her wish at this late date."

He made a face, and she didn't blame him. Her reasoning sounded very weak. But he hadn't heard the vehemence in Margaret's voice.

"Margaret never did get over Stuart deserting her, that much is true," he said. "There were vicious gossips who wondered if Margaret might have discovered Stuart and Priscilla eloping that night and shot both of them in a frenzy of jealousy. Colonel Randolph had taught Margaret to target shoot with a .22 pistol, so I suppose it's possible, but my father calls the idea nonsense. He believes Margaret is too gentle a person to ever resort to violence."

"What do you believe?"

"I think Stuart knew his parents wouldn't want him marrying his adoptive sister, so he simply left with Priscilla and the diamond brooch."

"And never contacted the family again?"

"'What would be the use?' he might have thought."

"I can understand his silence at first, but what about after his parents were dead? Stuart must have known your father would have welcomed him back."

Justin shrugged. "I don't pretend to understand what went on in Stuart's mind all those years ago any more than I understand what goes on in yours, here and now." The amber eyes blazed down at her.

Alida took a step backward and found herself up against the trunk of a pine. Attack is the best defense, she reminded herself. "You might as well pack up your tent because—"

"No way. I intend to camp here until you come to your senses."

"And what does Renée think of that arrangement?" Her voice was tart.

"She has nothing to do with us." As he spoke, Justin advanced, putting an arm to each side of her, his hands flat against the bole of the tree. "I'm rapidly losing my patience, Alida. What's wrong? Do I frighten you?"

She shook her head. The intensity of her feeling for him *did* frighten her a little but not Justin himself. His nearness confused her thoughts. Why was he doing this when he knew she'd seen him with Renée? He had no business saying Renée had nothing to do with them.

He couldn't have meant she'd become more important to him than Renée. Or could he?

"Alida, you've bewitched me, there's no other word for how I feel when I see you." Justin's voice was husky. "What's between us is so strong I can't keep from touching you, from wanting to be with you constantly." His forefinger traced the outline of her mouth.

I wonder, she thought. I wonder if Stuart said similar words to Priscilla when he should have been thinking of Margaret.

When Justin's lips covered hers everything fled from her mind but him and the passion he evoked within her. She couldn't think, she could only feel. There was no tomorrow, only the now here in Justin's arms. She was finished fighting her own need.

His fingers caressed her breasts through the cotton of her top, then slipped underneath the cloth. She'd left off a bra because of the heat, and the touch of his hand on her bare breasts made her moan with pleasure.

Her tongue tasted the sweetness of his mouth, more delicious than any food, more intoxicating than any drink. She breathed in his erotic male scent, her fingers on his bare back felt the ripple of his muscles, steel under satin as he slid his hands down to cup her buttocks, molding her to him.

Knees trembling, she clung to him in breathless rapture. This was the man she'd waited for since she was a child, the only man she'd ever wanted with all-consuming desire.

He drew away a little and eased her down onto the brown pine needles underneath the tree, at the same time sliding her top up over her head, letting it fall to the ground. The needles were cool and soft against her skin, while her breasts tingled against the curls of Justin's chest hair.

His tongue trailed along her throat and down, down, finding one nipple and then the other in velvety caresses that left her gasping. She held his head to her breasts, her fingers tangled in his golden hair.

"Justin," she whispered. "Oh, Justin."

His hands stroked the sensitive skin of her inner thighs, easing under the edge of her shorts. The smoldering conflagration within her blazed out of control and she arched against him. A thrill of anticipation shivered through her when she felt his need for her.

His lips at her ear murmured, "My little gypsy, my Alida, you're lovely, so lovely."

How could she do anything but hold him close as delicious warmth blossomed in her loins, a pulsing need that only he could bring to fruition. She longed to feel him against her, no clothes barring the way, yearned to make him a part of her, to become a part of him, the two of them one.

Improbably, the faint scent of roses came to her, intruding into her erotic trance. Alida opened her eyes.

A dark figure stood near the tent, staring at her and Justin.

Alida drew in her breath, struggling to free herself, to sit up.

"What's wrong?" Justin asked huskily, tightening his grasp.

"Mrs. Danford!" she gasped.

Six

―――

Justin released Alida and she sat up, grabbing for her top. By the time she had it on and looked back at the tent, a flutter of black disappeared into the trees. Mrs. Danford was gone.

"Where is she?" Justin demanded, on his feet.

"She was by your tent. Watching us." Alida tried to smooth her hair but nothing could ease her tangled emotions.

Justin strode to the tent and came back with a bright red rose in his hand. Alida recoiled as though the rose were a snake.

"I can't believe she climbed all the way up here from the gatehouse just to bring you that rose," she said. "Mrs. Danford doesn't like me, she hasn't from the first time she saw me. I think she's spying on me. Maybe she's the one who set the fire."

"Mrs. Danford?" Justin's laugh was incredulous. "Why would she do such a thing?"

"Well, KHI will be turning her out of the gatehouse eventually. She might resent that."

"Out of the gatehouse? But that's impossible. She owns the gatehouse."

Alida stared at him. "You're wrong. KHI is buying the entire parcel, all the McLeod land, including the gatehouse."

Justin shook his head. "Mrs. Danford owns the gatehouse and the land for a hundred feet on each side."

"Why didn't your father tell us?"

"I wasn't aware he hadn't."

Alida glared. "I've been over the papers a hundred times. The gatehouse was supposed to be included in the deal."

"Did my father say so specifically?"

"I don't know. Certainly we assumed he knew what he was doing, what he owned and didn't own."

"You should have asked him."

"I disagree. He should have excluded the gatehouse and the land he sold to Mrs. Danford from the agreement."

Justin's amber eyes turned cold. "My father is perfectly competent," he snapped, "but he's not in the business of buying and selling property and KHI is. You're trying to cover up your own mistake."

"We made no mistake! As for you, you didn't want KHI to acquire the estate anyway."

"What in hell are you talking about? I didn't care if my father sold to men from Mars as long as he was sure in his own mind he wanted to give the place up."

"That's not the way I heard—"

"I seem to have arrived in the nick of time." Renée's coolly amused voice made both of them whirl.

Renée was dressed in white riding breeches and a pale lavender shirt. She tapped a crop against her boots as she glanced from Alida to Justin. Not a strand of her blond hair was out of place. She looked absolutely stunning.

"I could hear you shouting from the house. A minute more and you'd have been at each other's throats. Justin, you poor boy, you need a ride on Thunder to cool down. I brought him up on a lead rope with Lightning." Her glance took in the tent, flicked to Alida and dismissed them both. "I took your boots out of your car when I passed it on the pullout halfway up. Why on earth did you leave the car there?"

For a moment no one moved or spoke. Alida's chin went up. "Enjoy your ride," she said, her tone suggesting she hoped Justin would break his neck.

Without waiting for either of them to answer, Alida marched toward the mansion, her stomach churning with anger and frustration. I could have told her why he left the car on the pullout, she fumed. He went to get his camping gear and then stopped partway up so I wouldn't hear or see the damn car this morning. Wouldn't know he was hiding in the woods. No doubt Renée will make short shrift of his plan to camp there.

Forget Justin. What are you going to do about the gatehouse?

By the time Alida reached the apartment she knew there was no choice but to call KHI and tell them what she'd discovered. Perhaps Justin was mistaken, though she doubted it. Still, she'd stop on her way down the mountain and talk to David about the gatehouse.

In the bedroom, Alida changed into a skirt and brushed her hair. She washed her face, scrubbing at her lips as though to erase any trace of Justin's kisses.

Before she left, she looked one more time for Lady, calling her, but the cat was nowhere to be found.

At the hunting lodge, Knowles told her Mr. McLeod was out and hadn't left word as to when he'd return. Alida decided to go on to Persis and call KHI anyway.

So much for plans to return to Arizona in the near future, Alida thought as she drove back up the mountain an hour later. Ken Hubbard was still in Switzerland, but his immediate superior had told her she was to stay in New York and solve the problem. As far as he was concerned, that meant coming back to Phoenix with the entire parcel in KHI's pocket, no matter who the gatehouse belonged to.

She'd called the hunting lodge before returning to her car, only to hear Knowles repeat what he'd already told her, so she'd left a message for David McLeod. But who knew when he'd receive it? Meanwhile, she was stuck in the Catskills. How was she to avoid Justin while she tried to clear up the problem of the gatehouse?

Alida didn't recognize the silver Mercedes parked under the porte cochere. Who was here? Someone to see her? She frowned in puzzlement and, instead of letting herself in the kitchen door, she went to the main entrance.

The front door was ajar. She pushed it open, walked inside, and stopped short in the foyer, staring in amazement at the man emerging from the library.

"Mr. McLeod!"

David had said he never meant to set foot in the place again and yet here he was. Alida watched him come toward her, her suspicions growing. Was his aversion to the mansion only talk, a smokescreen to cover other visits here? Had he been coming to the mansion secretly?

Why?

If he had, though, he could have been responsible for the fire. How quickly he'd insisted a backpacker caused it. Too quickly, perhaps?

As for the gatehouse, he must have known all along that KHI assumed it went with the rest of the property. What kind of a game was he playing? She'd thought him a lonely and rather sweet middle-aged man, but it began to look as though David was far more complicated than she'd imagined.

Unless—was it possible he could be slightly deranged? Forcing herself to remain perfectly still, Alida swallowed as David walked up to her.

"I knocked at the apartment door but you weren't home, as I expected when I didn't see your car." He sounded quite ordinary but his face was pale and strained, his eyes haunted.

"I went to call on you."

He didn't seem to hear her.

"I want you to go upstairs with me," he went on. "I can't make myself go up there alone."

Alida tried to smile. "Maybe I could go upstairs and do whatever it is you want instead."

"No. If I don't do this myself it'll be useless. I've been pacing about down here trying to work up the courage. You'll think I'm a strange person, a grown man who can't face the second story of his own house."

She didn't reply because he was right, she did find it odd, and she felt sorry for him. Still, she had her own obligations to fulfill.

"Would you answer one question first?" she asked.

"A question?"

"About the gatehouse. Do you own it?"

"No. Beatrice Danford does. I sold it to her seven or eight years ago."

"KHI wasn't aware of this."

David blinked. "I supposed the lawyers had told them."

"Evidently not. It creates a problem."

"Offer Mrs. Danford a good price—she hasn't much money, she'll probably be glad to sell. I stopped and talked to her when I came up today and thought she looked terribly unhealthy. Her face was gray and her lips almost blue. It must be hard being so isolated. I shouldn't have sold her the gatehouse in the first place, but she was set on owning it, kept pestering me, saying she wanted to be by herself where she could grow her roses."

Mrs. Danford must have overexerted herself climbing to the mansion earlier, Alida thought. No wonder her lips were blue. That was a steep hike for a young woman with two sound legs, and Mrs. Danford was not only far from young but she limped. *I hope he's right and she does want to sell.*

"We really do need the gatehouse," she said. Since the building's so unusual, KHI planned to use it for an information center. "I assume there's indoor plumbing?"

David nodded. "I remember when my father put in the septic tank and leach lines. It was during that July when Stuart left. The workmen had just finished the day Randolph's house burned." He closed his eyes briefly. "I can't forget. Everything that happened then is etched in my mind forever."

Alida eyed him nervously, recalling how Justin had mentioned his father hadn't been well. At the moment he looked ready to collapse.

"Are you sure you want to climb the stairs?" she asked.

"I must."

She certainly couldn't prevent him, but she could go with him as he'd asked her to in case anything did happen.

"I'm ready to go when you are," she told him.

He took a deep breath and let it out slowly. "Now or never." With an apologetic smile, he held out his hand to her and after a second's hesitation, she took it.

Holding hands, they climbed the wide, curving staircase, Alida feeling a sense of unreality about what she was doing, as though she was moving in a dream.

When he stopped at the top of the stairs, his hand trembled in hers. Gently, she urged him forward and after a moment's resistance, he followed.

"Where are we headed?" she asked.

"Her room." The words were almost a whisper.

There was no need to ask who he meant. Priscilla's room, of course. She ought to have realized that's where he'd go.

The corridor darkened as they walked along and a frisson of uneasiness trickled along her spine. Storm clouds hiding the sun, she assured herself. Thunderheads have gathered on the mountain every afternoon since you've been here. Remember—that's how the mountain got its name.

The rational explanation did nothing to ease her growing apprehension. What was she doing in these dim, decaying halls hand in hand with a man who behaved as oddly as David McLeod?

The air of the second floor was suffocatingly hot and oppressive. She found it hard to breathe. Glancing sideways at David, she saw his face was set and grim. Hardly reassuring.

By the time they reached Priscilla's door her nerves were on edge, and tension coiled within her. She started violently when a board creaked underfoot.

David let go of her hand and stopped, facing the door. Instead of being relieved that he wasn't touching her, she missed the human contact, however small. His hand shook as he plunged it into his pocket and he almost dropped the key he finally brought out. He fumbled at the lock, struggling to insert the key.

"She's fighting me," he mumbled.

The hair rose on Alida's nape at his words.

As the key clicked inside the lock, thunder rumbled in the distance. David looked at her as if to say, you see?

Get this over with! she wanted to cry. Hurry!

David turned the knob of the unlocked door, paused, then suddenly shoved it open. The door swung inwards to crash against the wall, making Alida gasp.

"There, damn you!" David shouted into the room.

Nothing was inside, it looked the same as all the other bedrooms. Stale dust-laden air drifted into the corridor.

"I should have done this years ago," David said, speaking not to Alida but to the empty room. "I should have exorcised you, Priscilla, instead of locking you in here.''

Alida fought her impulse to flee down the stairs and out the front door.

David stepped into the room. She edged forward, standing in the doorway, reluctant to follow him.

"The floor," he muttered. "Look at the floor. She's been in here, I see her footprints."

Eyes wide in mixed horror and disbelief, Alida fixed her gaze on the uncarpeted floor where footprints of a woman's shoes crisscrossed the dusty boards.

"She had tiny feet," David said, his eyes unfocused. "Her shoes looked like they'd fit a child. But she was far from childlike. Priscilla was what men in those days called a pocket Venus." He took a deep breath, staring once again at the footprints, then swinging around to face Alida.

"No, no," he cried, "she didn't make those footprints, they're too large to be hers. She's not here, only memories of her were locked in this room." He pointed a finger at Alida. "It was you, wasn't it? You got in here somehow and walked across the floor. You did it, she sent you here to haunt me."

Alida shook her head frantically, unable to force words from her dry throat as she stared at David's agonized face.

A door slammed downstairs. Alida screamed and David jumped back. A moment later he rushed toward her. Before she could move, he'd shoved her aside and was running toward the stairs.

On trembling legs, Alida hurried after him, anxious not to be left alone near Priscilla's room. She reached the head of the stairs in time to see David opening the front door.

A draft had slammed it shut, she told herself. When he opened Priscilla's door it must have created a draft, that's all. A draft.

David left the front door wide open and before she reached the foyer she heard the motor of his car. When she reached the porch, the Mercedes was speeding down the drive. Lightning streaked from sullen gray clouds, a rumble of thunder following belatedly.

Alida drew in a deep breath, realizing she was reluctant to turn and cross the foyer to her apartment. What was she afraid of? An empty house? Certainly there was nothing inside it to fear. David's reaction to unlocking Priscilla's door may have unnerved her, but he was gone, and she had no unpleasant memories of that poor war orphan to exorcise.

I'm going to march right back up those stairs to that room, she told herself. It's the best way to rid myself of any lingering trace of fright. Like getting back on the horse that's thrown you. After all, I may be staying here for longer than I thought, and I'm damned if I'll let fear of an empty room chase me to a motel.

In the pre-storm light the staircase was shadowed, the upper corridors dim and gloomy. Alida strode toward Priscilla's room with grim determination, her footsteps echoing on the bare floors, passing the closed doors of the other bedrooms. When she reached Priscilla's room, Alida pulled the door shut abruptly. The sharp sound of its closing reverberated up and down the hall.

More slowly, she returned to the stairs and descended to the foyer. She hadn't enjoyed the trip upstairs but it had served a purpose. The residue of David's fear and anguish was banished from her mind.

Since she didn't care to drive into Persis to have dinner in a restaurant, she ate a light supper alone in her apartment. Lady Luck was nowhere to be found, and she worried about the cat spending the night outside. She thought of the owl and the other predators in the woods, and tried to console herself with the fact that if Lady had survived this long the chances were she'd make it through one more night.

After eating, she tried to read but couldn't concentrate. Would David's outburst against her this afternoon cause him to change his mind about selling? Surely when he calmed down he'd realize she couldn't possibly have gotten inside that locked room, and so the footprints couldn't be hers.

Whose were they?

Alida shook her head. Don't borrow trouble. Perhaps the former caretakers had a master key to all the rooms, it seemed likely. The footprints had undoubtedly been made then. Certainly they weren't Priscilla's. She hoped David would see this when he finally came to his senses.

If he ever did.

Tomorrow she'd sound out Mrs. Danford about leaving the gatehouse and push as hard as she could for the sale. Probably David had been right in thinking the old woman needed money.

It occurred to her she'd also committed herself to having lunch with Margaret Randolph. She had to drive into Persis anyway for more supplies if she meant to stay on, so stopping at The Ferns for lunch would be no problem.

As long as she didn't run into Justin and Renée again.

She could no longer keep him out of her mind. He came alive in her memory—tall and tanned and virile, amber eyes glowing, mouth curved in a tender smile. She closed her eyes, once again feeling his hands caressing the curve of her hip, she tasted the delicious thrill of his kiss, the scent of his body filled her nostrils. She formed his name with her lips. Justin....

Alida's eyes flew open. This would never do. Determinedly, she went to her portfolio and removed the McLeod estate papers, the maps of the resort-to-be, everything she'd brought from KHI. She pored over the material until finally her eyes drooped sleepily. By ten o'clock she was in bed.

She was in darkness. She had no name, no identity and knew nothing of where she was. Hands groping in front of her, she searched the dark and found only four walls and a locked door. A room. She was locked in a room.

Rattling the knob and pounding at the door brought no help. Terror struck at her. What if no one ever came to let her out? She hugged herself, discovering her nakedness, and shivered in fearful desperation.

Suddenly she wasn't in the room, she stood instead in a dimly lit hall. A closed door loomed in front of her. On its other side someone cried to be let out.

"Please, please," the woman inside wailed.

Alida tried the knob but the door was locked and she had no key. The prisoner's words degenerated into mewing noises as she wept behind the door. Alida, knowing it was Priscilla, was gripped with agonized pity, but there was no way to help her.

Priscilla was locked in that room for eternity and no one would ever release her. Her piteous cries wrung Alida's heart.

Alida woke with tears on her cheeks, her heart pounding. She sat up, looking around a bedroom lit by the comforting glow of the night-light. Dreaming. She'd been dreaming of Priscilla. Dreaming Priscilla was locked in that upstairs room...which, now that she thought about it, must be almost directly over this bedroom.

A thin wailing widened her eyes and her hand flew to her mouth. What was she hearing?

In the dream Priscilla had wept over her imprisonment but now Alida was awake. Not dreaming. Had she imagined she'd heard that cry?

She listened and it came again, faraway and plaintive.

From overhead?

Alida rose, took the lantern from the dresser and went into the kitchen where she unbolted the back door. Frogs and katydids serenaded the all-but-full moon. What she'd heard wasn't outside. She closed and rebolted the door.

Hesitating at the door to the foyer, she finally shot back the bolt and opened it. After a moment she heard the wailing again, a thread of sound, eerie and compelling. Hair rose on the nape of her neck. She was tempted to slam the door shut and lock herself into the safety of her apartment.

Nonsense. She didn't believe in ghosts. Whatever made that noise was alive.

Summoning her courage, Alida took a firm grip on the handle of the lantern and edged through the door into the darkness beyond. She swept the lantern's beam over the foyer. Empty. At the foot of the stairs she paused, listening.

Yes, the cry came from upstairs. Holding the lantern high, Alida started up, driven by the need to prove to herself she wasn't afraid of apparitions of darkness—they didn't exist. Only the solid and tangible existed, and that she could deal with.

Yet gooseflesh rose on her arms and her heart thudded in her chest. She fought against giving way to instinctive fears carried over from childhood of the dark and the unknown.

When she reached the top of the stairs the wailing grew louder. She followed the sound down the corridor that led to Priscilla's room, her bare feet noiseless on the cool wood of the floors. She paused to listen at one closed door after another, but the cry was always ahead. As she'd been half-aware from the first, she was being summoned to Priscilla's room.

What would she find inside?

Seven

———

All Alida had to do was open the door. Turn the knob, push the door inward. Her right hand gripped the handle of the lantern and as she willed the fingers of her left hand to unclench, nightmare pictures flashed before her.

The movie when she was eleven—a boy on the screen changing before her eyes from a handsome teenager into a creature from the tomb, dead for eons.

Beardsley illustrations in a book of her mother's— skulls lurking in the faces of beautiful women.

Stephen King's alive yet long-dead horror in the bathtub at that isolated western mountain hotel.

She tried to swallow but her throat was too dry.

Imaginary monsters, she attempted to tell herself. There's nothing like that behind Priscilla's door. She's gone from here, she left years ago. If she's dead, she's buried in her grave. She's not here, not in this house. No part of her is here, no ghost, nothing.

Yet something was on the other side of that door.

I can't do it, she thought. I can't open the door.

Do you intend to run back downstairs and cower behind your bolted doors, a still rational part of her mind asked. If there really are monsters, what's to prevent one from coming through the wall of the apartment when you think you're safe? You've never believed in such things and you don't now. Where's your backbone?

Alida's hand shot out and twisted the doorknob. With a quick thrust she shoved the door inward. Lantern held high in front of her, she stared into the room.

And saw nothing. She released her pent-up breath in a whoosh. At that moment something furry brushed against her bare ankle and she yelped, nearly dropping the lantern. Staggering back to the opposite wall of the corridor, she caught sight of a small black and white bundle of fur.

"Lady!"

The cat mewed, following her, twining about her ankles while she sagged against the wall in relief. Alida reached down and picked up the cat. Lady began to purr.

"Was it you crying in Priscilla's room? How did you ever get in there?" She cuddled the cat to her breast and started for the stairs.

Alida took three steps, then stopped. She'd opened the room, she'd found Lady, but she still hadn't actually gone inside. Taking a deep breath, she turned and retraced her steps.

"I'll bet you came in behind David when he left the front door ajar," she said to Lady, finding reassurance in the sound of her voice. "You went upstairs and later I shut Priscilla's door, trapping you inside. Right? Poor Lady, you're not so very lucky today."

Carrying the cat, Alida entered Priscilla's room, telling herself she'd made a quick survey so she'd be positive it was completely empty.

A board creaked under her foot, sagging alarmingly. Alida tried to jump to one side but the board cracked and broke and her foot went through to the subflooring underneath, the splintered board scraping her leg.

Setting cat and lantern on the floor, Alida pushed aside the broken board to release her foot. Lady promptly leaped into the hole.

"No!" Alida cried. "Come out of there." She reached in, groping for the cat, and her fingers closed over something hard and oblong. She lifted it into the lantern light. A book bound in green leather—no, not a book, "My Diary" was written in flaking gilt on the cracked leather.

Lady peered from the hole. Alida collared her and, cat and diary tucked under her arm, hurried back to her quarters, thankfully bolting the door behind her.

She fed the hungry cat, thought about going back to sleep but realized she was too keyed-up. In fact, she felt positively euphoric. Hadn't she conquered her fears, located Lady, and found what might be Priscilla's diary all in one fell swoop?

With pillows propped behind her, she sat in bed, the cat curled at her feet, the diary unopened in her lap. A tingle of anticipation ran along her back. Did she hold the answer to the mystery of the McLeod past in her hands?

Slowly and carefully, Alida opened the cracked green cover. "Priscilla Tudor," she read in flowing script, the ink brown with age. She frowned. Why did the writing look familiar to her? Shaking her head, she turned the page.

"I hate it here," she read. "Mother and Father McLeod feel sorry for me but they don't love me. Nobody does."

Poor displaced Priscilla. An outsider here. Like me.

Alida read on, smiling over Priscilla's gratified surprise when the boys at the local high school began hanging around her locker and fighting to sit next to her in study hall.

"None of those boys matters to me, though," Priscilla wrote. "They're so silly. I prefer older men like S. If he'd only notice me. Somehow I have to make him see me as a woman, not a little girl."

S. was Stuart, of course. Why had he succumbed to this schoolgirl?

"Everyone says M. is the prettiest girl at the high school," another entry said, "yet the boys don't trail after her like they do me. M. is always hanging around our house, she even plays those boring games with D., just to keep in S.'s good graces, or so she hopes. I hate her."

Alida frowned at Priscilla's graceful script, still bothered by the nagging sense she'd seen this handwriting before. Suddenly she dropped the diary, waking up the cat who yawned and shifted position.

It can't be, Alida told herself. Priscilla's handwriting is almost exactly like my mother's. Why hadn't she seen that immediately? Her mother wrote beautifully, with a graceful, flowing script. So did Priscilla.

The bedside lamp flickered and she heard the growl of thunder.

The handwriting is only similar, she assured herself, closing her eyes in an effort to make the picture of her mother's handwriting clearer. She opened them and glanced at the diary.

"Priscilla Tudor," the first page proclaimed.

No, it couldn't be. Her mother's name had been Catherine Drury née Wakefield. Memories of the time sixteen years ago when she'd lived in this mansion with her mother flooded her mind and she shivered.

Mother had acted strangely that summer. Alternately excited and sad. At the time she'd thought her mother's moods had something to do with the books she was cataloging—never read books to be sold to others who might never read them, her mother had said, calling it a terrible waste.

Was that the reason? Or had her mother been concealing the truth?

David McLeod had been away the entire time she and her mother had stayed in the mansion. Had her mother been afraid David might return and recognize her? Recognize Priscilla?

Nonsense. Her mother wasn't Priscilla. Impossible!

Was it?

Why had David believed her to be Priscilla when he first saw her? Alida knew she looked like her mother, people had told her that all her life.

Who was there to tell her the truth? Her father, Drake Drury, had died when she was a baby. A chill ran along her spine as she realized that if her mother had been Priscilla, it was probable her father would have been Stuart McLeod.

No! She didn't believe it.

But who was there left to ask? Her mother, orphaned as a child, had died two years ago. Alida had been told she had no living relatives. She'd never questioned the fact until now. Other people had uncles, aunts, cousins, yet she had none. It seemed strange.

Frantically she searched her memories for any shred of evidence that her parents couldn't have been Priscilla and Stuart but could dredge up nothing that might prove they were or they weren't.

Her father was only a picture to her anyway, a black and white photo of a solemn, good-looking young man.

"Golden hair," her mother had said. "Eyes like sherry."

As for her mother, the memories telescoped one into another, but Alida could form no clear recollection of her mother as a young woman and didn't remember seeing any early photos of her. There'd been no wedding pictures.

"There was only your father and me, no other relatives, so we didn't make a fuss about getting married," her mother had said.

Dark hair and eyes. Like Alida herself. And like Priscilla.

Near dawn she slipped into an uneasy sleep.

Lady's impatient meows woke Alida. She glanced at her travel clock and saw it was almost noon. Remembering her lunch date, she scrambled from the bed, let the cat out and hastily showered and dressed. After lunch she intended to finish reading the diary and also speak to Mrs. Danford about selling the gatehouse.

As she drove through the outskirts of Persis, the fire whistle hooted. When she'd been a child here that was the signal for the volunteer firemen to rush from their homes or jobs to the fire station and roar toward the fire in the shiny red engine. As she recalled, Justin and his freckle-faced friend had planned to volunteer as soon as they were old enough.

She listened and looked for the engines as she drove into Persis, heard distant sirens and decided the fire was on the other side of town.

Margaret was seated at a table beside the planters at the restaurant, sipping white wine. "I'm delighted you could come," she said.

Alida ordered a Chablis from the hovering waitress and smiled at Margaret. "It was kind of you to ask me."

"I suppose you're wondering why I did, why I want to talk to you."

"It crossed my mind."

"I don't really know why. When I heard you were staying at the McLeod mansion I felt a compulsion to meet you and, oh, I'm not sure how to tell you without you thinking I'm a total nut, but I want to explain to you so you'll know how it was once. With Stuart, I mean. Don't ask me why—perhaps I'm getting to be terribly eccentric as I age."

Alida murmured a polite denial, her sympathy engaged and her curiosity as well. Maybe Margaret could cast new light on the McLeod mystery.

Margaret fumbled in her shoulder bag and brought out a photograph, handing it across the table to Alida. For a moment Alida thought she was looking at a picture of Justin with a blonde young woman, then she realized the photo was yellow with age.

"Stuart and I, when I was a senior in high school."

Alida glanced from Margaret to the picture, then back, seeing traces of the pretty young woman in the photo—the high cheekbones, the tilt of the head. But the girl in the picture shone with happiness while an aura of sadness surrounded Margaret.

"Stuart looks very much like Justin."

Margaret nodded. "I was eighteen then, in love and certain a wonderful life lay ahead for Stuart and me. He was four years older and had been a pilot in the Army Air Corps. I thought I'd never feel worse than I did the day I heard he'd been shot down over Holland. I was wrong." She gazed into her almost empty wine glass.

"I did hear Stuart was wounded, then discharged from the service," Alida put in.

"The army doctors didn't think he'd ever be able to resume a normal life, but once he came home he recovered rapidly and seemed whole again. We'd played tennis in the summers ever since I was thirteen—he went to prep school, so I didn't see him much except in the summer—and he used to treat me like a younger sister. Anyway, he called me when he came home from the hospital and all that winter of my senior year we dated. I'd always been in love with him, and I was ecstatic when he told me he loved me." Margaret's gaze was faraway, there was a faint smile on her face.

"Then she came. Priscilla." Margaret frowned and fell silent.

"Priscilla arrived around Christmas, didn't she?"

Margaret didn't seem to hear. "For awhile nothing was different. I'd be over at the McLeod house playing games with Stuart and his little brother, David, while Priscilla looked on. I even felt sorry for her, losing her parents and all. I defended her in school when some of the girls made fun of her English accent.

"I should have seen then how determined Priscilla was, because by May she hardly had a trace of that accent left. Oh, yes, Priscilla worked hard to get what she wanted." Margaret glanced at Alida, her brow furrowed. "She was a dark little thing. Quiet, but somehow she stood out. The boys certainly noticed her, though we girls didn't think she was particularly pretty."

"I've seen a picture of her."

"Looking back, I think Stuart began to change toward me in early May. By the night of the senior prom he was definitely different. He was my date, of course. How I'd looked forward to that night and showing off Stuart. We weren't officially engaged but I wore his prep school ring on a gold chain around my neck. My evening gown was a beautiful shade of powder blue, and Stuart brought me the loveliest corsage of tiny white roses. Roses were his favorite flower, you know."

Alida watched Margaret's face soften and change, grow younger. "I remember every detail of that night. At first everything was perfect . . ."

Stuart pinned the rose corsage on Margaret's blue tulle gown with the vee neckline she thought was rather daring. His fingers accidentally brushed the bare skin between her breasts, and her heart pounded as a sudden thrill transfixed her. He was so handsome in his tuxedo he took her breath away.

"That dress is the same color as your eyes," he said and she smiled at him, feeling as though she were floating on clouds as he escorted her to his gray Packard coupé with the whitewall tires.

At the high school gym, every eye was riveted on them as they entered. Margaret could see the envy in the other girls' glances, and she knew the boys all admired Stuart—he was a war hero, after all. She felt very special to be the choice of such a wonderful man.

Margaret had hoped he'd fill her dance card with his name, saying he didn't want to dance with anyone else. That wasn't like Stuart, however, and he didn't. She danced with other boys, basking in their admiration, aware she was as beautiful this night as she'd ever be, aglow with her love for Stuart.

It was while she was dancing with Burt Yates, captain of the football team and Priscilla's date, that Margaret had her first tremor of doubt. The band was playing "Careless," a slow number, and when Burt tried to pull her closer, she resisted, keeping what she thought was the proper distance between them.

Priscilla, though, was nestled against Stuart in a way that disturbed Margaret. Especially since Stuart gazed so intently at Priscilla's upturned face. He was so bemused he didn't even see Margaret when she and Burt danced past. A lump of ice formed in her stomach, chilling her. She watched him after that and to her distress noticed that even when he danced with her, his eyes searched for Priscilla.

At first glance Priscilla's gown was nothing special, though the color was a brilliant pink. Passionate pink, Burt had called it, and laughed in his suggestive manner. The long satin dress was rather plain, with none of the ruffles Margaret's had. The neckline was high, and she hadn't thought the dress daring until she saw how it clung to Priscilla as she moved, outlining breast and hip and thigh in a way that drew the eye of every boy in the gym.

Margaret was too upset to feel jealous, too confused by the way Stuart was acting. He scarcely said a word to her between dances. When the prom ended he took her directly home instead of stopping at one of the after-prom parties. His goodnight kiss was perfunctory.

In her room, she flung herself onto the bed and wept until no more tears came. She got up and took off the blue tulle, washed her face, then, about to put on her pajamas, stopped. She had to talk to Stuart now, tonight. Not on the phone, she couldn't face the thought of waking Mr. McLeod and asking to speak to Stuart. Yet she couldn't wait until tomorrow. Her parents were asleep, they wouldn't know if she crept out and went over to the McLeods'.

Stuart's room had a balcony. If she couldn't attract his attention by throwing stones at the balcony, she knew the McLeod storage shed had ladders. Her heart thundered at the idea of climbing into Stuart's bedroom in the middle of the night—no decent girl would do a thing like that! She was desperate, though. She couldn't wait until morning to find out what was wrong between them.

With the aid of her flashlight, she followed the path through the woods, wearing navy blue slacks and a wine blouse so she'd blend with the night. As she threaded through the trees, the flashlight's glow grew dimmer and dimmer until it finally blinked out.

Margaret stopped. The half-moon's light didn't penetrate the gloom under the trees and she was afraid to continue for fear of getting lost. Besides, how was she ever going to find the nerve to go into the McLeods' shed and haul out a ladder, prop it against the balcony and climb up? She was sure to make noise and get caught. Her face burned at the thought of what her father would say.

What had seemed simple in her own bedroom now loomed as an impossible task. She sighed, not wanting to wait until tomorrow, but knowing she couldn't go on.

As she turned to grope her way back home, a girl's laughter floated on the night breeze. Laughter that teased and beckoned. She heard a male voice respond, though she couldn't make out the words. Margaret knew without a shadow of a doubt it was Priscilla. With Burt Yates? Yes, of course it must be Burt. No business of hers. But Margaret found herself heading toward the sounds.

They weren't far away. In a tiny clearing, at the base of a tall pine, she saw not Burt's dark hair but Stuart's golden curls gleaming in the moonlight. Priscilla stood before him, her pink gown sliding from shoulders silvered by the moon. Stuart flung off his jacket and shirt and reached for Priscilla who evaded his grasp, laughing. Until at last he caught her. Margaret watched them fall to the ground in each other's arms, and heard Stuart say hoarsely, "God, I can't get enough of you, you damn little gypsy."

She turned and fled, blundering through the trees, not caring where she was headed, her dreams in ruins, living the scene over and over in her mind. By some miracle she came out of the woods near her house and managed to get to her room without rousing her parents.

The next day she mailed Stuart's prep school ring back to him. A week later, in the post office, she met Priscilla who smiled sweetly and held up her left hand. On her fourth finger, wrapped with tape to make it fit, was Stuart's ring.

"I wanted to die for awhile," Margaret told Alida. "I even imagined how sorry Stuart would be when he heard I'd killed myself over him. Of course I didn't have the nerve. Instead, I've lived all these years, and he's the one who's dead."

Alida stared. "You know Stuart's dead?"

"He must be. Otherwise he'd have gotten in touch with David by now. He knew how his little brother idolized him. Stuart wouldn't have hurt his brother, he was too kind-hearted."

"Did you ever speak to Stuart again after that prom night?"

"No. He called me on the phone once or twice but I told my mother I wouldn't talk to him. What was there to say?" Margaret's blue eyes, faded now from the powder blue they once had been, narrowed. "It was her doing, I see that now. Priscilla's. If I'd had any sense I wouldn't have retreated. I was what was called a nice girl. She wasn't. I didn't stand a chance and neither did Stuart, despite being older. I'm sure she forced him to run away with her. She wanted him all to herself, didn't intend to share him with his parents or with poor David. The only thing I can't understand is why he left without a word. I don't mean to me, but to his family, especially to David. It wasn't like Stuart, not like him at all."

Tears filled her eyes. "I loved him so," she said brokenly. "I still do. I've never loved anyone else before or since." Sobs shook her shoulders.

Alida looked away, giving Margaret the chance to get control of herself. Her glance went to the table Justin and Renée had occupied the night she met him here.

Justin and Renée. Stuart and Margaret. Yet Stuart didn't marry his Margaret. The outsider took him away, Priscilla won Stuart. Then what happened?

Did Stuart change his name to Drake Drury? Did Priscilla change hers to Catherine? Why? Because they took the diamond brooch when they eloped?

The diary might give her a clue. She had no other way to find out.

"I'm sorry to behave so foolishly," Margaret said. "I've never told anyone the entire story of that night before. I've often longed to talk to David about it, but I don't believe he'd want to hear. In fact, I don't go near him, though I've always been fond of David and I miss seeing him."

"From what he's said to me, I got the impression David's fond of you, too."

Margaret shook her head. "I'm afraid I'd only remind him of the past." She took a deep breath. "Somehow I knew you'd understand and be sympathetic. It seems as though we've known one another for years, not just days. I feel better now but I didn't mean to break down like that."

"I'm sorry the past is so painful still," Alida said.

"You see, I believed Stuart loved me. He told me so. And he meant it. I think now he didn't love Priscilla. Yet he went away with her. Went away, leaving me alone."

Alida left the restaurant feeling sorry for Margaret. How sad that she'd let herself be trapped in the past. Stuart had a lot to answer for.

As soon as she entered her apartment, Alida headed for the bedroom. Until she finished reading Priscilla's diary, everything else would have to wait, KHI included. She had to find out all she could about the little English girl who'd destroyed so many lives.

The diary wasn't on her bedside stand where she thought she'd left it. She looked on the floor and under the bed. Nothing.

Alida frowned. She didn't recall putting it anywhere else. A search of the bedroom didn't turn up the diary. It wasn't in the living room, the kitchen, nor in the bathroom.

The diary wasn't in the apartment.

Yet it certainly had been when she left to drive into Persis. Where had it gone?

Eight

If the diary wasn't in the apartment, then someone had taken it. Who? Alida put her hand to her mouth. How had they gotten in?

Justin and his father had the only keys. Did David believe she was Priscilla's daughter? Had he set the fire to frighten her away?

Wait. There was no proof her mother had been Priscilla, only a wild suspicion in her mind. She could be all wrong. It was time to set aside her speculations and finish the job she was sent here to do. Then she could leave. All personal concerns were just that—personal. She'd come here on business.

Get it done. Then leave.

Never mind who has the diary or wants you away from here. Forget Justin. Finish your job and go. Don't become trapped in the past as Margaret Randolph is.

Thunder rumbled as she set off for the gatehouse. Clouds were massed overhead again. The perpetual threat of a storm had her on edge, and she wished the storm would break and get it over with.

The scent of roses surrounded her as she got out of the car. Stuart's favorite flower, Margaret had said. Alida knew she'd never smell roses again without remembering her time here. Nor see brown-eyed susans without thinking of Justin.

She tapped at the gatehouse door, a thick panel of pine. Mrs. Danford opened the door a crack, peering out at her.

Alida smiled, "You remember me, don't you? Alida Drury—I work for Kentin Hotels and I'm staying at the mansion. I wonder if we might talk."

"What about?" Mrs. Danford's voice was harsh and suspicious. She didn't open the door any wider.

"My company is interested in buying the gatehouse, which I understand you own. I can offer you a very good price."

"No! I don't want to sell. I'll never sell the gatehouse. To you or anyone else. Go away from Persis. Leave the big house before it's too late. You shouldn't be there. It stirs up things."

"Mrs. Danford, if you'll just—"

The door slammed shut, cutting off her words. Alida heard the lock click inside. She took a deep breath. Of course she'd have to try again later, but Mrs. Danford's attitude was certainly not encouraging. Shoulders drooping, Alida turned away from the gatehouse.

Before she reached her car, Justin's gold Ferrari roared into the drive and pulled up at the chain. He leaped out, grinning at her.

"Ready for our picnic?" he asked.

"Whose picnic?" She managed to keep her tone cool despite the erratic flutter of her heart.

"The one I'm taking you on."

"I've already had lunch."

"Then we'll eat late. Or you can watch me eat. No problem. Surely you know food is only part of the reason for a picnic."

Despite her vow to avoid Justin, she found herself saying, "What're the other reasons?"

"To be outside. To enjoy nature with a congenial companion."

"You're a congenial companion?"

"Voted the most congenial man in southern California last year. Care to see my certificate?"

Alida smiled, she couldn't help it any more than she could stop her pulse from accelerating when Justin was near her. Yet it would be the height of folly to yield to her desire to be with him.

"I really can't take the time to—"

"Of course you can. What's more important, that's what you have to consider. How could anything be more important than enjoying this beautiful day?" With you, his eyes added, holding hers, hypnotizing her with their amber glow.

Beautiful? The day was hot and muggy, the ever-present thunderheads massed above the mountain.

"Come with me, Alida," he said softly and she was lost.

As she settled herself in the Ferrari she saw a picnic hamper in the back. "What would you have done if I'd turned you down?" she asked.

He touched her hand. "You couldn't. We're both under a compulsion to be with one another—don't say you haven't felt it."

She stared at him, surprised and discomfited. A compulsion from the past, is that what he meant?

The Ferrari roared down the mountain, the breeze in her hair pleasant and refreshing. Alida pushed away thoughts of the past and the future. She wanted to be with Justin and she meant to enjoy her time with him. One way or another, she'd soon be gone from here, this interlude with Justin would be over forever.

A pang gripped her heart at the thought of never seeing him again, and she blinked to keep back tears.

"I heard the fire whistle when I drove into Persis," she said, to get her mind off the future. "I remembered you always wanted to be a volunteer fireman."

"I became one. I still join them when I'm visiting Persis, but today I got there too late to help. A bad blaze—it destroyed a bakery and two fireman were injured. What were you doing in Persis?"

"Having lunch with Margaret Randolph."

"After suspecting her of starting the rag fire?"

"I gave that up. She wouldn't have. I feel so sorry for her. She loved Stuart, and she's never forgotten him."

Justin sighed. "My uncle and Priscilla messed up a lot of lives."

"And I don't believe for one minute that Margaret killed them. She couldn't do such a thing."

"Every one of us is a potential murderer, given the right circumstances."

Alida shook her head.

"Why is it we never agree on anything?" Justin asked. "I'd prove to you I'm right but today's too hot to argue."

"You claimed it was a beautiful day."

"Isn't it?" He grinned at her.

She smiled back, knowing what he meant. Being together made any day beautiful.

"It's going to rain, though, before tonight. My father says there was a ring around the moon and a mackerel sky last night—infallible signs."

"Won't you get wet in your tent—or have you given that up?"

"I moved it, but I'm still around."

He must be on the other side of the house, she thought, or he'd have seen the light from her lantern last night and come to investigate. And probably have scared her to death, she'd been so jumpy. She'd never once thought of Justin camping in the woods while she was creeping up to Priscilla's room.

"Anyway, the tent's waterproof," he pointed out.

It was on the tip of her tongue to remind him he could always put his sleeping bag inside the mansion but she bit the words back. Wouldn't that be an invitation in a way? Two of them under the same roof?

Warmth rose inside her as she contemplated rain beating down in the night and the two of them in each other's arms . . .

Stop doing this, she told herself. There's no future in a relationship with Justin. Have you forgotten Renée?

After a time Justin turned onto a dirt track, drove a few yards and stopped at a wire fence. On the other side of the fence pine trees grew, row on row.

"I don't see a gate," she said.

"There isn't one. Don't worry about it." He came around to open her door but she'd already let herself out. He collected the hamper and led the way to a break in the fence wide enough to slip through. She went through first, and he handed her the hamper, then followed before retrieving it.

The pines closed over their heads as they walked on, a soft breeze whispering through the branches. The woods were ordered, not like the haphazard growth on the mountain. Either the dense shade of the trees prevented undergrowth or the brush had been cleared away.

"They planted these pines around Ashokan Reservoir years ago, sometime before 1920," Justin said. "The dam across the Esopus was finished in 1913. Twenty-three million, it cost. Cheap by today's standards."

"My mother told me once there were towns where the waters of the reservoir are now."

"Seven villages, a railroad and a couple of cemeteries."

"All under water?"

"They moved the graves and some of the houses. Everything else was drowned by the waters of Esopus. Eight thousand acres went under. When I was a kid some of the oldtimers used to tell stories about the Mafia coming up from the City and dropping people into the concrete when the dam was poured."

"What a really romantic picnic site."

He smiled wryly. "Just trying to impress the out-of-town folk. I mean, it isn't Hoover Dam and Lake Mead, but 'tis mine own."

They came from under the trees onto a rocky ledge that dropped away toward blue water sparkling in the sun. Across the lake pines bristled along the water's edge with blue hills stretching beyond.

"They say there was a preglacial lake here at one time, it seems a natural site for water to collect," he said.

"It's beautiful. Can we go down to the shore?"

"Not right here, we'll have to backtrack a little."

He led the way onto a promontory where the ledge sloped more gently to meet the water. Gravel covered the rock just above the water line. Alida stood at the very edge gazing into the clear water. Beneath the surface she made out dark rock falling away into hidden depths farther out. Some distance from her a post thrust upward under the water, almost but not quite reaching the surface.

Part of a submerged village fence? The post moved and she shook her head. It must be a log washed into the lake during a storm.

Alida saw her own reflection and Justin's, who stood behind her. There was no sign of drowned villages. The lake had hidden them in its dark depths as the secrets of the past were hidden from the present. Yet the houses were still down there somewhere, unseen yet remaining.

As the past remains to haunt the minds of those still living.

Were she and Justin re-enacting the past? Was she coming between him and Renée just as Priscilla came between Stuart and Margaret?

She saw his hands move, felt him draw her close, her back against him, and knew she didn't care whether it was right or wrong, the feeling between her and Justin. The electricity his touch generated shorted out her mind, preventing her from thinking rationally.

"What's it like under the ocean?" she asked, leaning against him.

"When you get down to about seven hundred feet, it's a deep, deep blue—about like midnight under a full moon. You can see but it's shadowy."

"Do you wear a diving suit?"

"No, we're inside a small craft called a submersible."

As he spoke, his warm breath teased her ear. His hands drifted up to cup her breasts and she felt her nipples rise in desire. He started to turn her toward him when thunder rumbled in the mountains behind them, though the sun was still out.

Justin let her go. "We'd better find a spot for our picnic." Picking up the hamper, he took her hand and led her away from the lake.

They walked through the woods until they came to a stream flowing lazily around boulders. Justin settled on a flat rock above the stream. Pines grew close to either side of the water, but a narrow verge of grass and small bushes edged the water. On the far bank a small brown animal sat up on its hind legs and stared at them.

"Woodchuck," Justin said.

His voice didn't seem to alarm the animal.

"He's certainly giving us the once-over," she commented. "Aren't woodchucks afraid of people?"

"Not very. His only worry is we might go and eat his grass."

The water was so low they could easily reach the other side by stepping from boulder to boulder, but the woodchuck, seemingly satisfied for the moment, dropped to all fours and began to feed.

"We could eat, too," Justin said.

She helped him set the food out on a red and white checked picnic cloth—three kinds of sandwiches, potato salad, cold chicken, plums and cookies. There was a thermos of coffee and one of iced tea.

"Enough to feed an army," she observed, taking a deep red plum.

"I told the cook I was hungry."

Alida bit into the plum, finding its red juice sweetly tart on her tongue. When she finished, she took the pit and, digging a small hole with a stick, buried it.

Justin raised his eyebrows.

"Maybe years later I'll come back and find a little plum tree by this creek," she said.

Justin rose, walked to the stream, filled a paper cup with water, returned and poured the water onto the earth covering the spot where she'd buried the pit. "*We'll* come back," he corrected her.

We. She looked away from him, her heart heavy. He knew as well as she did that once she left the Catskills they'd never meet again.

The day darkened abruptly, and Alida looked at the sky where dark clouds had mounted high enough to hide the sun. Lightning zigzagged from the clouds toward the top of the mountain. Thunder echoed from the surrounding hills.

"Sounds close. We'd better hurry." Justin began repacking the picnic basket.

A cool wind blew down the creek as Alida folded the cloth and laid it in the hamper. Justin closed the basket. A rushing sound came from upstream, growing louder as it neared them, the sound of rain slashing through the trees.

"We'll make a run for it," Justin said, grabbing her hand and angling away from where she thought the road was.

"Aren't we heading toward the lake?"

"We don't have time to get to the car."

A large drop of rain struck her face. Thunder growled, seeming to come from all around them. Justin's hand tightened on hers and she ran faster to keep up. She had no idea where he was taking her, but a sense of exhilaration buoyed her as they tried to outrace the storm.

And failed. In a deafening burst of thunder the rain caught them, drenching them in seconds with its torrential downpour. Alida lifted her face, savoring the coolness after so many days of pre-storm heat.

Justin pulled her under a large outcropping of rock, a natural shelter formed by the ledge above them and the pines on either side. Brown needles were piled underfoot. She stood close to Justin in the small space, pushing her wet hair from her face and wringing water from it. Her soaked shirt and skirt clung to her body, but the storm hadn't brought cold air with it so she didn't feel chilled.

A bolt of lightning lit up the world outside their shelter, and the crack of thunder came from directly overhead, startling her. She was safe here, however, shielded from the storm, enclosed in a private little world with Justin.

She saw he'd noticed how her clothes clung to her curves and felt her nipples tauten as he looked at her breasts. His forefinger ran lightly over one, then the other, making her breath catch.

"Alida." His voice was a husky whisper.

She reached to him and his arms went around her. His lips claimed hers, urgent and seeking. She pressed close, holding his head to her own, answering his kiss, her tongue meeting his and entwining in a dance of passion.

She felt the warmth of his body through his wet clothes and an urgent demand rose in her to be free of the sodden cloth between them. She wanted the intoxicating touch of his bare flesh against her own, and her hands pulled his shirt away from his back to slide underneath.

Justin released her and yanked his T-shirt over his head. His fingers opened the buttons of her shirt one by one, then slid it from her shoulders. He unhooked her front-opening bra, his touch fueling her rising excitement.

Holding her away from him, he gazed at her bared breasts before caressing them with both hands, at first gently, then more urgently. She moaned when his mouth replaced his hands, delicious flashing thrills piercing her loins.

He held her close again, his hands stroking her back and the sides of her breasts. Thunder rumbled and reverberated, a vast crescendo of sound matching her inner tumult—the pounding of her heart, the storm of desire mounting inside her.

She had no place to run to now, but she no longer wished to. She was where she wanted to be, where she needed to be, where she belonged—in Justin's arms. She felt the hard demand of his body against her and knew his need was as great as her own.

This is the time, the place, her senses clamored. Here among the pine needles, sheltered from the rain by the rock in a secret place that satisfied some deep yearning she'd never known she had. It excited her to think of them being outdoors and yet hidden. Of experiencing the storm without discomfort. Of coming together in this pine-scented niche belonging to them alone.

Alida's hands went to the fastening on her skirt. Moments later she and Justin had shed the rest of their clothes. His gaze traveled over her body, his amber eyes aflame with desire.

"Beautiful," he murmured. "My beautiful, bewitching gypsy."

Alida stared at his wide shoulders, the muscular torso that narrowed at his waist and thought him beautiful, too. She caught her breath when she saw his aroused manhood, a molten river of passion rushing through her.

He lifted her into his arms and knelt, still holding her, his glorious golden eyes dilated with his urgent need. His mouth covered hers, kissing her as he gently lowered her onto the pine needles and eased down beside her.

Once again the aroma of the pine mingled with Justin's unique masculine odor. She knew she would never again smell pine scent without remembering, without thinking of Justin and this radiant, sensual moment.

If only it would never end. She wanted to lie in his arms into eternity.

Alida ran her hands over his chest, the golden hair springy under her fingertips, seeking the buds of his nipples. She wanted to touch him everywhere, to give him the intense pleasure his touch brought to her.

His tongue traced a warm erotic path along her throat and down, circling each nipple until she cried out with longing. She'd never imagined such rapturous languor mixed with a wild demand for fulfillment, never dreamed any man could create such a need within her.

The responsive skin of her inner thighs quivered under his fingers and she gasped as he touched her velvet softness.

"Justin, oh Justin," she breathed.

Torrents of delight flooded through her, penetrating her loins. She wanted him now, this moment, and tried to pull him to her.

Justin resisted, the caresses of his tongue and fingertips driving her frantic with passion. She flung her head from side to side, gasping for breath, moaning, calling his name.

"Look at me, gypsy girl," he murmured.

Alida gazed into eyes that were as warm as the sun, compelling her to unfold and open to him like a flower when he poised himself above her.

She closed her eyes as his hardness found her moist softness, overwhelmed by the throbbing rapture piercing her. Arching to him, she moved in the instinctive rhythm of love, a counterpoint to his deep and powerful thrusts.

Pulses of electricity shot lightning bolts of ecstasy through her, she was drowning in a cloudburst of thunderous sensation.

Justin called her name hoarsely and she clung to him, crying out as she tumbled with him in a wild, surging cascade of release.

Nine

Is it possible I could be Justin's cousin? Alida asked herself as she sat in her living room with the cat in her lap. She couldn't think coherently, her mind seemed to skitter and whirl like a waterbug on a pond. No matter how she tried to order her thoughts, she always came back to Justin.

They'd left their refuge when the rain slackened. He'd driven her back up the mountain, both of them silent and preoccupied. Alida couldn't talk because she feared if she opened her mouth she'd blurt out she loved him, that she'd loved him ever since she was ten. She didn't know why Justin didn't speak, but she was determined not to embarrass both of them by an outpouring of emotions.

Love hadn't been mentioned during those passion-filled moments under the rock ledge, and he didn't speak of love on the way home.

"I'll be back tonight," he told her when he stopped by the gatehouse chain so she could drive her own car the rest of the way.

Mrs. Danford, puttering among her roses, kept glancing at them. Alida tried to tell herself that's why Justin's parting kiss had been so brief and unsatisfactory.

Face it, girl, she thought. Your life may never be the same after what happened, but to Justin the lovemaking was no more than a pleasant interlude. Remember he made absolutely no commitment before or after.

"He'll be back tonight," she said to Lady, stroking the cat's soft fur. "I'll be with Justin again in just a few hours."

Lady opened her eyes and yawned, her pink tongue curling in her mouth. Already she'd begun to thrive on love and food—her coat glossier, her thin body beginning to round out.

Alida sighed. She could bring Lady back to Phoenix, but what about Justin? She was a fool to involve herself so deeply with him in a one-sided involvement she was bound to regret. How was she going to get through all the lonely days without him once she left the Catskills?

But, oh, those moments in his arms. Warmth rose in her as she relived the feel of his lips, his caresses, his body next to hers. She shifted restlessly and Lady dug her claws into Alida's leg to avoid slipping off her lap.

"Ouch!"

Lady gave her an indignant look and jumped to the floor where she set about grooming herself.

Here I am looking forward to more moments spent with Justin, Alida thought, when I should be concerned about the best way to tackle Mrs. Danford again about selling the gatehouse. KHI and my job are important to me. Already I've been promoted twice and if I pull this off...

Yet how could she keep her mind on business when Justin would soon be with her again? At the moment he filled her entire universe.

By ten that night Justin hadn't returned and Alida decided to go to bed. She was not only sleepy but didn't want him to think she'd waited up, though that's exactly what she was doing. She, who'd long ago made up her mind never to wait around for any man and who never had. Until now.

Perhaps he wasn't coming back to the house but instead was returning to the tent. Had he said he'd actually *see* her later? No. She'd merely taken it for granted.

Resisting her impulse to venture out and find his tent, Alida undressed for bed. As she slid under the sheet, she thought she heard the faint far-off moan of the fire whistle, but the sound wasn't repeated when she cocked her head to listen.

Finding herself lying wide awake in her bed, tensely waiting for Justin's knock, Alida pounded her fists against the mattress. She had to stop this. Immediately.

Think of your job, she admonished herself. Tomorrow you'll have to talk to Mrs. Danford again about selling. Maybe an indirect approach will work. You can point out the advantages of living closer to civilization and try to be subtle about the whole thing.

If only Mrs. Danford liked her better. From the first moment they'd met, the old woman's enmity had been obvious. Was it because Mrs. Danford, too, had thought she resembled Priscilla?

Alida drew in her breath. If it were true, that would mean Mrs. Danford had known Priscilla from somewhere. She shook her head. Except for the fact the old woman disliked her, all this was supposition.

If I'd read the diary I might have a few other facts to deal with, she told herself. Why didn't I at least skim through it instead of reading only the first few pages?

Thinking of the missing diary reminded her that someone had gotten into the apartment when she was gone. Who knew she had the diary? She'd certainly told no one. Again she found herself tensing.

Extra keys won't let an intruder in while you have both your doors bolted, she assured herself. You're perfectly safe. Lady climbed onto her stomach, curled up and began to purr. The soothing rumble relaxed Alida, and at last she drifted off to sleep.

She awoke some time later, certain she'd heard a door shut. The cat was alert, staring toward the open bedroom door. Alida sat up, listening. Was that faint creaking someone climbing the staircase?

Justin? she wondered. He might have decided to sleep inside the mansion with the woods so wet. Her heart speeded. She rose and picked up her lantern. Unbolting the door to the foyer, she poked her head out.

"Justin?" she called. "Is that you?"

No one answered, and she heard no unusual sounds.

Lady edged past her feet and darted into the foyer.

"Come back here!" Alida ordered.

Lady paid no attention, disappearing in the direction of the stairs.

"Oh, no!" Alida groaned, thinking of the trouble she'd had retrieving the cat the night before.

She stepped into the foyer, lantern held in front of her. "Lady," she coaxed. "Here kitty, kitty."

At the staircase she found unmistakable paw prints in the dust on the steps. Were the prints new or from yesterday? She had no way of knowing, for she hadn't thought to check the steps before. She raised the lantern. "Kitty, kitty?"

Lady didn't appear.

With one foot on the lowest step, Alida hesitated. Had she actually heard a door shut earlier or had it been in a dream? She turned and walked rapidly to the front door.

Locked. No one had come in.

Back at the stairway she started up confidently. There'd been no one in the house last night except herself and Lady, there was no one here now. She'd collar Lady and make sure the disobedient cat didn't get out of the apartment and into the mansion again.

Though she wasn't as nervous as she'd been the previous night, there was something intimidating about climbing the stairs into the dark. No matter how she held the lantern, its glow did little to illuminate the top of the staircase. When she reached the second-floor landing, she flashed the light down the first corridor. At least all the bedroom doors were shut, she'd have no trouble locating Lady.

"Here kitty, kitty."

Was that a faint mew to her left? Alida started to take a step in that direction, then swung around when she heard a hiss in back of her.

Lady stood near the top of the stairs with arched back, her fur standing straight up.

About to chide the cat for being afraid of her, Alida realized Lady was staring not at but past her. Hair rose on the nape of her neck.

The cat spat again. Thoroughly alarmed, Alida looked over her shoulder.

Something moved. With the lantern in front of her, Alida couldn't tell what Lady saw, but she flung herself toward the cat, away from whatever was hiding in the darkness. As she lunged ahead, a blow struck her back, pushing her toward the stairs. She cried out, stumbling sideways to teeter on the edge of the top step.

Managing to recover her balance, Alida fled down the staircase, the lantern banging against her hip. She shoved through the door to her apartment, Lady scooting between her feet, slammed it behind her and shot the bolt.

Turning on every light, she searched her apartment. No one, nothing was hidden there. Legs trembling, she sat on the edge of a chair, staring at the bolted door.

Someone had tried to shove her down the staircase!

The cat twined about her ankles and she picked her up, cuddling her to her breast. "You saved me, Lady," she whispered, her eyes never leaving the door. "What did you see? Who?"

The cat began to purr, her fright over and forgotten, but Alida's alarm mushroomed. If she'd fallen down the stairs she might have been killed. Certainly she'd have been seriously injured.

Who would want to harm her? And why? She couldn't see why she'd be a threat to anyone.

Had an intruding stranger been in the house and feared being caught? Where was her attacker now? Waiting outside her bolted doors? Alida shuddered.

No one can get in, she reassured herself.

Somehow she didn't think a stranger had attacked her. If not, though, who had it been?

David?

The last time she'd seen him his behavior had been distinctly odd. He might be normal in other respects, but speaking to the empty room as though Priscilla could hear him was unnerving. Then he'd accused her of being Priscilla's agent, sent to haunt him. Certainly a strange and unsettling way for him to act. Could he be so demented he'd tried to kill her?

Or had it been Mrs. Danford? She didn't like Alida being in the mansion and had warned her to leave. But surely the old woman was aware Alida would soon be going. There was no way of knowing why Mrs. Danford had taken such an instant dislike to her, no telling whether the dislike was personal or merely because she'd come to stay in the mansion. It seemed unlikely Mrs. Danford would try to push her down the stairs for such a trivial reason. Anyway, the old woman wasn't supposed to have a key.

Who did have access to the keys besides David?

Justin.

Nonsense. He'd made love to her earlier, the most thrilling and beautiful experience she'd ever had. She was no threat to Justin. And yet . . . he had a key.

How about Margaret Randolph? Had she kept a key from the old days? Even if she had, Margaret would have no reason at all for wishing Alida dead.

Renée's the only other person who might want me gone, Alida thought. I can't see her taking such drastic action, though.

Was the attempt on her life connected with the missing diary? She hadn't read much of it, but whoever had taken it from her apartment couldn't know that. They might believe she'd read the diary from cover to cover.

What was in it? Had Priscilla written words that would damn somebody?

Alida took a deep breath. She had no idea who'd waited for her in the darkness at the top of the stairs. She still had to try to persuade Mrs. Danford to sell the gatehouse. She couldn't leave the Catskills now, but as soon as it was daylight she meant to pack and quit the apartment for a motel.

As the drawn blinds began to lighten, Lady leaped off Alida's lap and headed for the kitchen door. Alida rose stiffly from the chair where she'd worried the night away. After letting Lady out, she rebolted the door and went into the bedroom, pulled one of her suitcases from the closet and opened it on the bed.

She soon had the cases nearly packed. Alida then went to the door and called Lady, but the cat didn't appear.

"You'd better show up," Alida muttered. "I might just leave without you." All the time knowing she wouldn't, that the cat depended on her and she'd no more desert Lady than leave a child behind.

By seven she'd finished packing and eaten breakfast. She called the cat again. Lady didn't come.

Locking the door behind her, Alida began a search of the grounds. Lady had certainly proved troublesome. On the other hand, she'd saved Alida's life.

"Here Lady," she called. "Come, kitty, kitty."

As Alida reached the verge of the woods, wondering if she'd spot Justin's tent, hooves pounded toward her. She turned and saw a beautiful palomino cantering toward her. On the horse's back sat Renée, her blond hair streaming behind her.

When she neared Alida, Renée reined in the palomino. In her silver riding outfit, she glittered as brightly as the diamond on her left hand. She looked down at Alida, her face cold, eyes hostile.

"Why don't you go back to Arizona?" Renée asked, words as brittle as ice. "You're embarrassing Justin by hanging around, don't you realize that?"

Alida said nothing, her mind in a turmoil.

Renée turned her horse and loped back the way she'd come, leaving Alida to stare after her. Could it have been Renée at the top of the stairs last night?

Alida finished her circuit of the ground without finding Lady or spotting Justin's tent. Dispirited, she returned to the mansion. To her surprise, Margaret Randolph waited on the side porch.

"I had to come," Margaret said. "I had the strangest dream last night. Stuart came to me, young and handsome, like he was the last time I saw him. He didn't speak, but somehow I knew he wanted me to talk to you again."

Alida did her best to be polite despite her own concerns. "Won't you come in?"

"No, thank you. I saw Renée on Lightning. What's she doing up here?"

"Looking for Justin, I imagine." The words were out before Alida could stop them.

Margaret nodded. "I thought as much. Justin means something to you, doesn't he? I sensed it at our first meeting."

Alida bit her lip. She didn't want to discuss Justin with Margaret.

"You don't have to tell me, I know because he's so much like Stuart. Who could resist him?" Margaret smiled sadly. "Don't give him up, Alida."

"I'm moving to a motel," Alida said sharply. "I have to go back to Phoenix in a few days."

"No. Don't go. Stay and fight. Fight for Justin. You love him, don't you? I didn't fight for Stuart, and Priscilla won. If I'd dug in my heels and stood up to her she wouldn't have gotten him, but I was too hurt and too timid. I did the wrong thing."

Alida blinked at Margaret's words. She'd thought of herself as the intruder, like Priscilla, and here was Margaret urging her to stay and fight for Justin. It was all very confusing.

"Margaret," she said hesitantly, "do I remind you of anyone you've known in the past?"

"No. Why?"

"I upset David McLeod when he first saw me. He seemed to think I looked like Priscilla."

Margaret stared at her. "Oh, no. No. You're not at all like Priscilla."

"She was dark," Alida persisted, "and small. So am I."

Margaret shook her head violently. "There's no similarity. David was mistaken."

"I can't stay here," Alida said.

Margaret sighed. "You'll be sorry all your life if you don't. As I've been."

"You and David should talk to each other," Alida said impulsively. "Thrash out the past and get rid of the ghosts. Together."

Margaret stared at her a moment, pressing fingers against her trembling lips, then turned and hurried down the steps to her car.

Alida watched Margaret's car vanish down the drive, then called Lady again with no results. Leaving her suitcase in the apartment, she drove to the gate-house, determined to give Mrs. Danford another try before she left the mansion. She parked near the chain and walked through the rose garden to the house.

The scent of the roses was cloying on the warm morning breeze, too sweet and heavy, almost suffocating. The flowers were beautiful, though, glowing pinks and reds from the palest shade to the almost black. Alida couldn't understand why she was so careful to avoid touching them.

She knocked on the gatehouse door and waited. No one answered. She knocked again. Still nothing. Either Mrs. Danford wasn't home or she had no intention of opening her door to Alida Drury. Giving up, she headed back to her car.

In the midst of the roses she stopped short, listening. Yes, she definitely heard a cat wailing, crying plaintively. Where was it? Alida looked around, spotted a shed behind the gatehouse. There. Of course it could be another cat, for all she knew Mrs. Danford might have one or more of her own, but she'd check it out just the same.

Calling Lady's name, Alida hurried toward the shed, stepping over a basket of garden tools left in the path. It seemed to her the cat mewed louder, as if recognizing her voice. "I'll let you out, pretty girl, don't worry," she said.

The shed door was padlocked and wouldn't open no matter how hard she shook and tugged at it. Convinced now it was Lady locked inside, Alida picked up a large rock and smashed at the padlock.

"Stop it, stop that, I tell you!" Mrs. Danford screeched from the gatehouse.

Alida turned her head and saw the old woman standing in her open doorway. Without replying, Alida brought the rock down onto the padlock once more and it sprang apart. She wrenched it off and yanked the shed door open.

Lady dashed from the shed into a stand of huge lilac bushes, disappearing under their green heart-shaped leaves.

"No, no, you have no right, none at all." Mrs. Danford rushed along the path toward the shed, dipping and bobbing because of her bad leg.

Alida, who'd started after Lady, paused.

"Mrs. Danford, Lady is my cat. *You* had no right—" She stopped abruptly, crying, "Watch out!"

The warning came too late. Mrs. Danford tripped over the garden tools and sprawled headlong onto the path, her legs among the rose bushes. She made no attempt to rise as Alida ran toward her.

"Are you hurt?" Alida asked.

The old woman moaned, her eyes closed, her face grayish. Her long black dress was rucked up and her right stocking torn. Blood oozed from a thorn scratch on her right calf. Alida was afraid to move her lest she make some injury worse.

What was she to do? Mrs. Danford needed help, but she wasn't strong enough to pick her up, put her into the car and drive to a hospital in Persis. Besides, moving her might be the worst thing she could do. On the other hand, she hated to leave her lying here while she drove to the nearest phone to call an ambulance.

Phone. Hadn't Justin once told her Mrs. Danford had a phone in the gatehouse?

In her rush to stop Alida from releasing Lady, the old woman had left the door open, so Alida hurried inside, her eyes searching for a phone.

The stone house had three rooms—kitchen, living room, bedroom—small but surprisingly uncluttered. Alida had expected to find the usual collection of the memorabilia of a lifetime, but Mrs. Danford had none. In her bedroom there was only a cot, a chest of drawers and a night stand on the bare slate floor.

Like a nun's cell, Alida thought as she reached for the phone atop the night stand. The ambulance number was listed in the front of the phone book.

"Be right out," the dispatcher assured Alida.

Retracing her steps toward the front door—Alida intended to wait for the ambulance by Mrs. Danford's side—she noticed a familiar book lying atop the kitchen table. "My Diary," the gilt letters spelled out across the cracked leather.

Alida stared at the diary, unable to believe her eyes. She picked it up, bringing it with her. How on earth had Mrs. Danford taken Priscilla's diary from her apartment? She must have keys the McLeods knew nothing about.

Outside, she knelt beside the old woman. With her eyes closed, Mrs. Danford looked somehow younger. Alida felt for the pulse in her wrist, found it weak and alarmingly rapid. She bit her lip, gazing down at the injured woman.

Was this who'd tried to waylay her at the top of the mansion stairs? Who'd started the rag fire? Mrs. Danford looked so small and pathetic lying among the roses that Alida couldn't believe it.

The faint wail of a siren rose and fell, becoming louder and louder as it neared. She rose to her feet.

"You did right not to move her," one of the paramedics said as they strapped Mrs. Danford to the stretcher. "Usually does more harm than good. You can follow us to the hospital so you can give the information and all. Okay?"

"But I hardly know her."

He shrugged. "Someone has to help fill out the papers and it's a cinch she can't."

The other paramedic adjusted the oxygen mask covering Mrs. Danford's nose and mouth. "Let's move it, Ray, you know what I mean?"

They thought Mrs. Danford might die before they got her to the emergency room, Alida thought in alarm. "I'll come to the hospital and do the best I can—" she began.

"Roses," Mrs. Danford muttered.

Alida walked beside the stretcher as the two men carried the injured woman to the ambulance. "I'll see that your roses are taken care of," she assured Mrs. Danford.

The old woman's dark eyes opened, focused on Alida, then grew bright with such malevolent hate that Alida stopped in her tracks, gooseflesh rising on her arms. Never before had anyone looked at her like that. The true meaning of "if looks could kill" came home to her with a shock.

There was no doubt in her mind that Mrs. Danford wished her dead.

Ten

Alida sat on a green plastic settee in the small hospital waiting room. Its only other occupant, a sharp-faced woman in her thirties, leafed through a *National Geographic*, but Alida was too upset to even try to read. When a nurse entered, she looked up expectantly.

"Larimer?" the nurse said.

"I'm his sister," the other woman announced, rising. She followed the nurse from the waiting room.

They'd no sooner left than a man rushed through the double doors, stopped short and stared at Alida.

"Justin!"

He strode to the settee, pulled her to her feet and took her in his arms. "I thought you were hurt," he said. "They told me an ambulance came off the mountain and I thought something had happened to you." He held her away from him, looking at her as though he wasn't yet sure she was in one piece.

"Mrs. Danford fell and hurt herself," Alida told him. "I don't know how badly, I'm waiting to hear how she is." Despite her concern for Mrs. Danford her heart was lightened by Justin's words.

"How did it happen?"

Alida told him. "And I have the diary in my bag," she concluded, reseating herself.

Justin dropped down beside her and she lifted out the diary, handing it to him. She looked on as he opened the green leather cover and again saw Priscilla's signature on the first page.

"I didn't read any more entries," she said.

"We can glance through it together while we wait." He put an arm around her shoulders and drew her closer to him.

It felt so right to be snuggled next to Justin. Savoring the warm closeness, Alida missed the first few entries as Justin rapidly turned the pages.

"S. watches me all the time now," Priscilla had written in March. "M. may think she's got him all wrapped up but she's wrong. I'm the one he looks at, I'm the one he wants even if he does keep holding back."

In April Priscilla turned sixteen. "I'm old enough to decide my own future," she wrote, "and it won't be as the McLeods' adopted daughter. I know what I want, who I want and I'll make it happen, see if I don't!"

"S. is taking M. to the Senior Prom," an early May entry read. "Burt Yates dropped Polly Pollard, the head cheerleader, to ask me to be his date. I think I'll go with him so everyone will notice and talk. If S. gets jealous he might do something exciting."

Again in May, "I can have any boy I want in the entire school without half trying. It's so easy. The trouble is I only want S. He kissed me last night on the porch!"

Later, "S. tries to avoid me but I'm not having any of that. When we're together he can't keep his hands off me. He's still dating M. but she's so prim and proper she wouldn't know what to do if he touched her like he does me. I've decided the prom will be their last date."

Entry after the prom. "I did it! S. is mine, now and forever. I love him, I really do, and he loves me, even if he hasn't said so. I can tell. Best of all, M. was creeping around that night and actually saw us in the woods though S. doesn't know that. She'll never talk to him again, that's the kind of girl she is."

"Margaret told me about that prom night," Alida said to Justin. "Finding Stuart making love to Priscilla broke her heart."

Justin nodded, turning the page.

The entries for June and early July were full of Priscilla's triumph over Margaret and how she relished showing off the ring she'd coaxed from Stuart.

I don't like Priscilla, Alida realized. A girl so petty and vindictive would mature into an unpleasant woman.

They came to the last entry, July twenty-sixth.

"That's my birthday," Alida said without thinking.

"Today?"

Her eyes widened. She'd been so distracted and disturbed by the events of the last few days she'd paid no attention. Today *was* the twenty-sixth of July.

Some birthday.

"S. says he loves M. and wants her back. Never! I'll make him pay for saying that. And her too. Tonight. I'll make him want me so much he'll forget her once and for all. I'd kill him before I'd ever give him up to that blond cow."

"That was the night of the fire at the Randolph house," Justin said. "The night Stuart and Priscilla disappeared along with the diamond brooch."

Alida took a deep breath. She had no proof Priscilla couldn't have been her mother, but she no longer believed it possible. Their handwriting might have been similar but her mother was a kind, loving woman who went out of her way to help others. Priscilla couldn't have become such a woman in a million years.

No, Priscilla wasn't Catherine Drury.

"I wonder why Stuart went with her?" Justin mused. "If he did. Too bad Priscilla didn't write just a little more."

Alida stared at the last words Priscilla had written. The faded ink showed a wider stroke than usual as though she'd transferred her fury to the nib of her pen.

"Danford?" A white-coated young man in the doorway asked.

Alida jumped to her feet. "I'm Alida Drury, the one who called the ambulance for Mrs. Danford. This is Justin McLeod."

"Dr. Jacobs." He stepped into the room. "Are you relatives?"

When they both denied it, the doctor frowned. "Does she have relatives you know of?"

Alida glanced at Justin.

Justin shook his head. "I'll ask my father but I don't think he's any better acquainted with Mrs. Danford than we are."

"I see. Well, the news isn't good. The fall she had didn't seriously injure her—a few scrapes and scratches—but she does have a serious heart problem. I've sent her to our intensive care unit and I hope I can stabilize her condition. At the moment she's in pretty bad shape."

"Then she'll be hospitalized awhile," Justin said.

"Definitely. Some weeks, at the least."

"I'll cover all her costs, doctor. Can we see her?"

"Since she has no family, I'd be inclined to say yes, but Mrs. Danford specifically asked that we allow no one to visit her." Dr. Jacobs turned his hands palms up and shrugged.

"Naturally we'll respect her wishes," Justin assured him.

Alida nodded.

"She's had this heart condition for some time," Dr. Jacobs said. "Do either of you know if she's been on any medication?"

"We wouldn't know," Justin told him. "Isn't Mrs. Danford able to tell you?"

"She's somewhat confused right now. We can hope that's temporary. After all, she's not quite sixty."

Alida stared at him. Mrs. Danford looked much older to her—in her seventies anyway.

Dr. Jacobs rose. "You may call ICU any time for a report on how she's doing." He nodded and went out.

"Don't be upset, Alida," Justin said. "Between my father and me, we'll see Mrs. Danford is taken care of, both in the hospital and after she's well enough to leave."

She smiled at him.

"I want you to do something for me now," he told her.

Anything, she was tempted to reply. Anything at all. Though she felt sorry for Mrs. Danford, she was warmed by Justin's presence.

"I'd like you to bring the diary to my father," Justin went on. "I'd go with you but I've something urgent to tend to, something that can't wait."

Renée, she thought, her euphoria fading. Renée is more important to him than anything else.

What did you expect? she asked herself. He made no promises to you.

"I'll be happy to take the diary to Mr. McLeod," she said.

And while I'm with David, she thought, I'll discuss the property sale and make certain he hasn't changed his mind. Then I'll pick up Lady and my bags from the apartment and head for New York City. With Mrs. Danford in the hospital I can't do any more here. I've stayed too long as it is.

She glanced at Justin, her heart heavy. "Goodbye," she said.

He moved toward her, stopping when a harried-looking man herded three small children into the waiting room. Alida turned and walked quickly out the door.

Though she half expected Justin to follow her, he didn't.

Switching on her car engine, she blinked back tears. It was over, their brief interlude. She still wanted Justin with all her heart and soul. How was she to bear his loss?

Knowles showed her through the lodge to the patio by the pool, where David sat in a lounge chair reading *The Wall Street Journal*. He laid the newspaper aside when she approached, waving her to a nearby chair.

"I've been formulating apologies," David said. "There's something about the old house that upsets me to the point where I don't know what I'm doing or saying. I'm afraid I said some unforgivable things to you the other day."

"I realized you weren't yourself." She pulled the diary from her bag. "I hope this won't disturb you—Justin asked me to bring it here. This diary was in Priscilla's room under a floorboard. I found it when the board broke."

David eyed the diary as though it were a bomb about to explode. "Priscilla's?" His voice was a whisper.

"Yes." She told him how Justin and she had read the diary while waiting at the hospital. "After the doctor informed us Mrs. Danford was in ICU and wanted no visitors, Justin thought you ought to have the diary. So I came here," she finished.

David took the book with hesitant fingers and opened it gingerly. "I recognize her handwriting."

"The last entry, on July twenty-sixth, doesn't reveal what happened that night."

"July twenty-sixth." David stared at the blue water in the pool, but Alida knew he was seeing the past.

"I've wondered ever since then if the fault might have been mine. Sometimes I wake in the night and torment myself by asking what would have happened if I'd done what I was asked to do. What if I hadn't lied about it, what then? Would everyone's future, including mine, have been different?" He sighed. "I'll never know."

Alida thought he might be blaming himself for events he'd had no control over, no matter what he had or hadn't done. He'd been only thirteen, after all, on that fateful night.

He sat in silence for a time, turning the diary over in his hands. Shreds of green leather flaked off and dropped onto his khaki shorts. Alida waited without comment.

"I lied to Stuart, you know," he said at last. "I've never admitted it to anyone, but I did. A lie of omission. I don't understand why to this day. I certainly wasn't afraid of him, he was always good-natured. Maybe it was the weather, we'd had a hot summer, like this one, with the rain holding off. Everyone was on edge—my mother, my father, Stuart and Priscilla. There was a tension in the house, in the way they acted. I felt left out...."

David hesitated outside the door to Stuart's room. He wanted to go in, but Stuart was at his desk writing and he didn't want to bother him. Music drifted from Priscilla's open bedroom door, Eddy Howard singing "Careless."

David wanted to drift past that open door and yet didn't want to. He pictured Priscilla brushing her long dark hair while she listened to the record on her phonograph. His face flushed as that picture of her was replaced by another, one he tried not to bring to mind.

It had been several weeks ago. He'd been asleep and something woke him, he never knew what. Once awake he was hungry, he always seemed to be hungry lately. Aggie, their cook, called him a bottomless pit. In his pajamas he tiptoed down the corridor toward the stairs, meaning to sneak down to the kitchen and raid the refrigerator.

It was after midnight and he was surprised to see Priscilla standing in her doorway, her eyes dreamy. The light was on in her room so that the outline of her body showed clearly through her sheer white nightgown—the pale curves of her breasts, the dark triangle of hair between her thighs.

He stopped, staring, he couldn't move or speak, all he could do was look at her, entranced, his body betraying how he felt.

Her eyes focused on him, flicked over him and she laughed, her high tinkling laugh that sounded like tiny bells. Laughing at him, at his helpless and frightened desire.

David had fled back to his room, her laughter echoing in his mind through the rest of a sleepless night.

No, he thought now, he wasn't going to risk another humiliation at Priscilla's hands. He didn't really like her. At the same time she fascinated him.

He clumped downstairs and across the back yard past the victory garden to the grape arbor where he found his football. For a time he played football with himself but he soon tired of it. He wished some of the other guys would come by. Most of his friends, though, were out of town with their parents or at camp.

He kicked a small, green windfall peach around the house to the front where he heard Stuart calling him from the balcony off his room. David ran.

"Here I am," he said, looking up at his brother eagerly.

"I want you to deliver a note for me. To Margaret."

David tried not to show his surprise. He knew Margaret and Stuart didn't go together anymore and suspected Priscilla had something to do with it.

"Sure," he said.

Stuart dropped a small sealed envelope and it fluttered down from the balcony, settling like a white butterfly in a pink rose of sharon blossom. David plucked it from the flower and slid the envelope into his pocket.

"Top secret," Stuart cautioned.

He nodded, Stuart saluted him and went back inside his room. David headed for the woods where the trail cut through to the Randolph house, wondering what Stuart had written in the note. Of course he'd never read it, he wouldn't betray Stuart's trust.

He reached the green gloom under the trees. It sure was hot. He wished a giant storm would hit, wind and thunder and lightning and rain, a real gullywasher.

"Davie! Davie, wait for me."

Priscilla's voice. No one but Priscilla ever called him Davie. He stopped, looking back, wary and excited at the same time. She hardly ever paid any attention to him, and when she did it was only to embarrass him in one way or another.

She wore white shorts and a red halter top. He tried not to look at the way her breasts pressed against the cloth of the halter. He really didn't think she was as pretty as Margaret, and she certainly wasn't as nice, but looking at Margaret never disturbed him like this.

"Where are you going?" Priscilla asked.

"Over to Randolphs'." It didn't occur to him to lie.

"I'll walk with you." She smiled at him.

"Well, uh, maybe you better not." He had to look down at her because she was so little that at thirteen he was taller. The halter veed in front showing the beginning rise of her white breasts and he couldn't take his eyes from them.

Priscilla's cool fingers touched his cheek. "You're growing up to be quite handsome, you know that, Davie?"

The way she said his name and the feel of her fingers on his face made him blush as excited apprehension coiled in him. She tucked her arm through his, her body pressing against him slightly. "Come on, let's go."

Speechless, unable to protest, he started off with her clinging to him. She began to hum the melody, then to sing the words of "Careless."

"Don't you just love Dick Jurgens' orchestra?" she asked.

David cleared his throat. "I kind of like Artie Shaw."

Priscilla leaned toward him so that her warm breath tickled his ear as she continued to sing. A delicious shudder jolted through him. One part of him wanted to pull away from her and run, while the rest of him waited, avidly expectant, for whatever would happen next.

"Why are you going to Randolphs'?" she whispered into his ear.

He jumped. "Uh, no reason. Just thought I would."

Priscilla smiled. "Stuart gave you something to bring to Margaret, didn't he?"

David stopped. "I better go on by myself."

She swung around so she was facing him, so close he could smell her perfume. Pink Clover it was. He'd seen the bottle on her dresser. Her nearness and the sweet scent made the blood pound in his temples.

"You're cute, Davie." She put her hands to his face, raised herself up and kissed him on the lips.

A riot of sensations battled within him, he could hardly breathe.

"Stuart wrote Margaret a note, didn't he?" Priscilla said, her mouth less than an inch from his. She pressed her body against him. "He did, didn't he, Davie?"

"Yes." The word escaped him, he couldn't hold it back, his legs trembled, he wanted, he didn't know exactly what he wanted, only that he wanted more.

"Let me see the note." The tip of her tongue flicked against his lower lip.

Sweat broke out on his forehead. "I . . . I can't," he gasped.

"Put your arms around me, Davie."

Slowly he obeyed, feeling the warm curve of her hip under his right hand, the bare skin of her back under his left. He couldn't think, could scarcely stand.

She kissed him again, rubbing against him, the delightful agony making him tighten his hold. Her hands ran down his back, along his thigh. Eyes closed, he moaned, swaying. He had no words to describe what was happening within his body, only knew it was wonderful and terrible.

Priscilla bit his lower lip with her sharp little teeth, hard enough to make him cry out in protest. She twisted free of his embrace and laughed.

"I've changed my mind about walking to Randolphs'. Thank you, Davie, thank you so much." Her voice mocked him.

He watched, frustrated and bewildered, as she turned and ran toward home.

It never occurred to him to check his pocket for the note until he emerged from the woods near the Randolph house. He reached for the note, found it gone. Searched all his pockets. No note.

David stood in the hot sun, angry and humiliated. Priscilla had outwitted him. She knew all along he had the note and had taken it from him before he'd realized what she was doing.

She'd made a fool of him. He swore at her, using all the curses he'd ever heard, while his body still tingled from her touch.

How was he ever going to explain to Stuart? Shoulders slumping, he started back home. Halfway through the woods, he paused. He couldn't face Stuart right now. Later, he'd tell him later. When he thought of what to say.

David spent the rest of the afternoon fooling around the pond. When he finally left the woods, Kevin McInerney was waiting for him on the lawn.

"Hey, Kevin."

"Where you been? I hiked all the way up here to show you what I got for my birthday. What d'you think of him?"

For the first time David noticed the brown and white puppy curled asleep at Kevin's feet.

"Wow. What's his name?"

"Prince. He's a purebred collie." When Kevin picked him up, the puppy squirmed in his arms, trying to lick his face. "You can hold him if you want."

The warm, wriggling puppy in his arms lightened the heavy lump in David's chest. He and Kevin played with Prince until Kevin's mother arrived in their station wagon to pick him up.

"Would you like to come into town and have supper with us?" she asked David. "I called your mother before I left and she said it was all right."

David quickly agreed. The summer twilight was darkening into true night by the time the McInerney station wagon delivered him to his own doorstep.

Stuart was waiting for him and took David up to his bedroom. "Did you go to the Randolphs'?" he asked.

David nodded. That much was true—he had gone there. He swallowed, nerving himself for the next question.

Stuart frowned. "I thought Margaret would call me by now. What did she—"

The moan of the Persis fire whistle cut off his words, and they hurried onto Stuart's balcony to see if they could spot the fire. The sky was aglow above the trees, and the acrid odor of smoke fouled the night breeze.

"Somewhere close," Stuart said.

"I'll go see where it is." David ran back through the bedroom and down the stairs as though fleeing from a fire instead of searching for one. He raced out the front door and across the lawn.

He didn't look back at the house. If he had he might have seen his brother on the balcony. Seen him for the last time.

"I never saw Stuart again," David said to Alida. "I've wondered for years what was in that note I didn't deliver. I've always wanted to tell Margaret Stuart he had written her a note, but I never found the courage. Seeing me could only cause her pain, and she's had enough hurt."

Alida, recalling that July twenty-sixth diary entry, thought she knew what the note said. "S. says he loves M. and wants her back." The trouble was that the wrong person read the note—Priscilla, not Margaret.

What had happened then?

Eleven

With David's assurance that the sale to KHI was still on, Alida left the hunting lodge, intending to drive directly to the apartment for her bags and Lady. As she was about to turn right onto the highway to head up the mountain, Alida hesitated, then made a left turn. She couldn't leave Persis without telling Margaret Randolph about the note Stuart had written her so many years ago on this date, the note Margaret had never received.

Margaret had said she lived in a condominium complex called White Clouds at the east edge of Persis, and Alida found the place easily. Perhaps she should have stopped to call ahead, but this wasn't something to be discussed over a phone.

"I'm sorry to show up with no warning," Alida said when Margaret opened the door to her ring. "May I come in?"

"Of course. I'm delighted you've come calling. I was afraid you'd left town for good."

"I'll be going before this evening." She followed Margaret into a living room that, to her surprise, was furnished in Danish modern. She sat in a blond chair with a vivid coral seat.

"I've never cared for old furniture even if I do live in the past," Margaret said, apparently sensing how Alida felt. "Would you like coffee? Tea? Lemonade?"

"Nothing, thank you." Waiting until Margaret had seated herself in a blue-cushioned chair, Alida went on. "I've just come from David McLeod. I think you should hear what he revealed about the day Stuart disappeared."

Margaret listened to the story of the note, hands clasped in her lap, outwardly calm, her only sign of tension the whitening of her knuckles as her hands clenched tightly together. When Alida finished, Margaret sat so long without speaking that Alida began to eye her nervously. Had she done the wrong thing?

"I'd like you to come with me," Margaret said at last. "You can follow me in your car. Please. I don't want to be alone."

Alida nodded agreement, though she had no idea of where Margaret meant to go.

Trailing Margaret's brown Aries, she soon realized they were headed up the mountain. She slowed as the Aries neared the gatehouse, thinking Margaret meant to turn in there. She didn't, driving on toward the old Randolph place.

Why? What could be left among those ruins?

Margaret pulled into the weedy drive far enough for Alida to park behind her.

"We can't take the cars any farther," Margaret said. "The road's overgrown."

Alida nodded, remembering the day Justin had brought her this way.

Margaret headed up the drive on foot and Alida followed her, threading between saplings, sometimes knee-deep in weeds. When they neared the ruins of the house, Margaret headed across a field gone back to wild growth. She didn't acknowledge Alida's presence in any way, and Alida suspected Margaret had forgotten she was along. Locusts shrilled all around them.

"There were locusts that year, too." Margaret paused, looking into the woods. "From here I could see the lights at McLeods', but now the trees have grown too thick. She went on, veering to avoid the stunted, decaying survivors of the small apple orchard.

Ahead of them Alida saw a low stone wall holding back the rise where the woods began. The wall, built of field stones cemented together, bulged outward in the center where many of the stones had fallen into the weeds. Margaret stopped, staring at the wall, her eyes scanning it as though searching for something. She nodded, walked past the bulge several feet, then halted.

"This was our place," she said. "Stuart's and mine. When I was thirteen he began leaving notes here asking me to play tennis with him."

A secret hiding place? What on earth did Margaret expect to find here? Not Stuart's note, certainly. Even if it had been left here in the wall, nothing would remain after all these years.

Margaret felt along the uppermost stones with her hand, pausing when she came to a gray one with white veins. She grasped the rock and pulled but it didn't move. Using both hands, she worked the stone back and forth while dirt and concrete particles spattered onto her shoes. The stone came free, and she dropped it to the ground to reach into the opening.

Alida watched in amazement as Margaret brought out a small case and placed it on top of the wall. Inching closer, Alida saw that the velvet cover was stained and torn, its original color blackened by mildew. The hinges were rusted away. Very carefully, Margaret lifted the cover.

Alida gasped and blinked as she gazed at two sparkling circles of diamonds with an immense diamond set between them. Even the gold of the setting was as yellow and gleaming as if the brooch had been hidden the day before.

Margaret picked it up, the diamonds glimmering, and held the brooch in her palm. Her eyes were faraway, her smile dreamy.

"It's beautiful," Alida breathed but Margaret didn't seem to hear her.

"He did love me," Margaret whispered. "Stuart loved me."

The note, Alida thought. That's what the note would have said. Something like: "There's a surprise in our hiding place. When you see it you'll know how I feel about you."

Because the McLeod brooch was what the eldest son gave to his wife. Leaving it there had been Stuart's romantic gesture, his declaration of love to Margaret. She was the woman he wanted to marry, not Priscilla.

Why, then, hadn't he stayed and married Margaret?

"I won't keep the brooch," Margaret said, gazing tenderly at the sparkling jewels. "It must go back to the McLeods."

"But Stuart meant you to have the diamonds. He left the brooch for you."

"I don't need the diamonds. By hiding them here, Stuart gave me something far more precious and valuable. The brooch isn't mine, it's meant to be for Justin and I'll bring it to him." She put her hand on Alida's arm. "You'll never know how grateful I am for your help. You've given me more than I can ever repay."

Tears gleamed in Margaret's eyes and Alida felt her own eyes water. She touched Margaret's shoulder. "I'm so happy for you."

"Stay in the Catskills. Find your own happiness here."

Alida bit her lip. Happiness wasn't for her. Not with Justin. "Take the brooch to David instead," she urged Margaret. "He wants to see you, he told me he did. You must talk to him."

Margaret blinked. After a moment she nodded. "Yes. I'll go to David. I'll go now."

Alida hugged her and stepped back. Later, alone in her car, Alida puzzled over why Stuart would go to the trouble of hiding the diamond brooch for Margaret, surely a proposal of marriage, and then run off with Priscilla.

Leave it, she told herself. Leave the McLeod past behind, the same as you're leaving Justin. It has nothing to do with you.

At the gatehouse she got out and called Lady. To her delight the cat dashed from under a boxwood hedge and ran to her.

"Oh, Lady, I couldn't have stood it if I'd lost you, too," Alida cried, picking up Lady and cuddling her.

With the cat beside her, Alida drove up the winding road to the mansion, her heart feeling heavier and heavier as she climbed. How could she bear never to see Justin again, never to feel his arms around her, never to be consumed by the blazing fire of his kiss?

The blue twilight of summer had settled over the mountain by the time the mansion came into view. Alida suddenly braked the car. She was almost certain she hadn't left any lights on. Yet a soft glow shone through the drawn shades of the apartment. Still, with all the upset, she might have forgotten, might be mistaken about what she had or hadn't done. She shrugged and continued on to park under the porte cochere.

Leaving Lady shut in the car, she approached the side door, key out and ready. She really didn't think anyone was in the apartment. It was obvious Mrs. Danford had been the one who took the diary from her bedroom, and she was in the hospital. About to insert the key in the lock, she paused. There was still the person who'd tried to shove her down the stairs in the night. What if that hadn't been Mrs. Danford? What if someone did wait for her inside her apartment?

Alida took a step backward.

Suddenly the door was flung open and she shrieked, throwing up her hands defensively.

"Happy birthday," Justin said.

Behind him the kitchen table, draped with white linen, was set for two, candles in silver holders flickering in the breeze from the open door. Justin bowed, gesturing with a sweep of his arm for her to come in.

She advanced slowly, unable to assimilate what she saw.

"Your table awaits, Ms. Drury," Justin told her. "Your wish is my command." He closed the door behind her.

"Oh, Justin," she said excitedly. "So much has happened. I didn't know what to think when I saw the lights. Where did you hide your Ferrari—behind the house? I can't get over you doing this. And, wait, you don't even know about the diamonds."

"You mean the brooch?"

She nodded.

"Sit down and I'll pour the wine while you tell me about it."

Alida sank onto the chair. "We found the McLeod brooch, Margaret and I."

"You what?" Justin almost missed the stemmed wine glass as he poured.

She told him how she'd listened to his father, then gone to see Margaret.

"And she opened that battered old jewel case and there was the brooch. Margaret's taking it back to your father."

Justin shook his head. "I don't know what to make of it. In a way I'd come to think of the missing diamonds as the McLeod myth."

"I wonder why Stuart disappeared after he left the brooch?"

"Enough of the past," Justin ordered. He finished pouring the wine and, sitting down, lifted his glass to touch hers. "To a happy birthday."

"It's certainly one of a kind."

The chilled Chablis was slightly tart on her tongue, exactly as she liked it. "Something smells awfully good. Are you acting as chef, too?"

"I make a fair waiter but I'm no chef. The cook at the lodge came up with a chicken and shrimp casserole she claims will melt in your mouth. I'm to serve it with a green salad and home-baked rolls."

Listening to him, Alida realized how hungry she was. No wonder, she'd had practically nothing to eat all day. "I can't wait, it sounds so delicious."

"We could have our wine with the meal."

"I'd like that."

"Don't get up from your chair, this is my party." Justin opened the oven, lifted out a gold pottery casserole dish and carried it carefully to the table. He brought the salad, tossed in a crystal bowl, from the refrigerator, took the rolls from a bun warmer.

Before he sat down, he turned out the kitchen overhead so the only light came from the candles. "I trust this suits Ms. Drury's romantic fancy," he murmured.

"Fantastic. You deserve a generous tip."

His eyebrows lifted. "I won't forget to claim it. Later."

Warmth that had nothing to do with the wine glowed deep within her. Tonight. She'd have tonight with Justin, never mind what tomorrow had to offer. Tonight she wouldn't think about yesterday or tomorrow.

When they'd finished eating, Justin cleared the table, poured coffee, then ducked into the tiny pantry. Moments later, he returned carrying a white frosted layer cake with twenty-six flaming candles.

"How did you know how old I was?" she demanded.

"I called KHI headquarters in Phoenix, what else?"

She shook her head at him.

He set the cake in front of her. "Make a wish."

Justin was the only wish she had.

"Ready?" he asked.

She nodded, took a deep breath and blew at the candles. Twenty-five went out, one candle still flickered. Before she could blow at it again, Justin pinched out the flame with his fingers.

"That's cheating," she complained.

"No. What it means is with my help you won't have to wait a year to have your wish come true."

You're my wish, she said silently. One that will never come true.

He removed a small, gaily-wrapped package from his pocket and handed it to her.

"A present? Oh, Justin, you didn't need to. All this and a present, too? I didn't expect—"

"Open it."

Inside the paper was a tiny hand-carved box with a hinged lid. She lifted the lid. Nestling in brown velvet was an exquisite enamel-on-gold pin of brown-eyed susans.

"Justin, I love it," she breathed, hardly able to speak. She held the pin in her hands, the delicate workmanship blurring as her eyes filled with tears.

She'd rather have this pin than the McLeod diamonds Renée would someday wear.

"I hoped you'd like the pin. It reminded me of you." He drew her to her feet, holding her loosely in her arms, smiling down at her.

She blinked back her tears. "You've made this birthday special."

His eyes took on a golden glow that made her catch her breath. Clouds of desire formed inside her, a prelude to the storm of passion only Justin could evoke.

"I've only begun," he murmured.

As he started to pull her closer she gasped and held him away. "I just remembered I left Lady shut in the car. Poor thing, she's already been locked in Mrs. Danford's shed for hours. I had to break the padlock to get her out so I suppose it's partly my fault that Mrs. Danford fell."

"I don't think I'm following this. What does the cat in your car have to do with Mrs. Danford's fall?"

She told him, adding, "I don't know why she locked Lady in the shed. Unless she was the one who tried to push me down the stairs last night."

"Whoa . . . who tried to push you down the stairs? You didn't tell me anything about that." His face was grim. "I wondered why your suitcases were packed, but I decided you'd come to your senses and were moving into a motel."

"I was afraid to stay here another night," she admitted, not telling him she'd planned to head for New York City.

"What were you doing wandering around the other part of the house at night anyway? There's no electricity, and the upstairs floors aren't that safe even in daylight."

"I heard a noise and I thought you might have moved into the house because of the rain. When I opened my door to the foyer to see if it was you, Lady got out and I had to retrieve her. I didn't know someone was upstairs until I felt hands on my back shoving me."

"You don't know who it was?"

"I couldn't see. I suspect it might have been Mrs. Danford because Lady's warning hiss saved me from a nasty fall and later she locked Lady in her shed. What other reason would she have for that?"

"I don't know. But why would she want to push you down the stairs? It doesn't make sense." He shook his head. "I must have slept through it all, out in the woods. So much for my job as watchman. Damn it, I should have slept in the house. I was going to but I was so late getting up here last night I was afraid I'd wake you by opening the front door and then scare you to death."

"Mrs. Danford doesn't like me. I don't know why." Alida turned toward the door. "I'll bring Lady in and feed her the scraps from the casserole."

"You stay here. I'll get the cat."

By the time Justin brought Lady into the kitchen, Alida had filled the basin with water and started on the dishes. She tossed Justin a towel. "Your turn to dry."

He grinned ruefully. "I had the evening planned differently. Ever since the day I met you in the library, you've been changing the course of my life. You're a high-handed, stubborn, impulsive person, Alida Drury."

"It takes one to know one. Dry the dishes, McLeod."

"Ask any of the guys I work with in California if I'm not a reasonable, easy-to-get-along-with type."

"Ask anyone in KHI if I'm not amicable and equitable," she countered. "You must bring out the worst in me."

"Not always." His eyes caught and held hers, twin suns that fired her blood.

With difficulty, she turned her attention to the dishes again, a thrill of anticipation tingling along her back and down her legs. Tonight, tonight was hers. Hers and Justin's.

"There," he announced, draping the towel over the back of a chair. Advancing, he scooped her up into his arms.

"Justin!"

"I've decided to let you bring out the worst in me, too," he growled, carrying her toward the bedroom.

Alida nestled her head against his chest, smiling when the rapid beat of his heart told her he was as excited as she. In the bedroom he slid her down his body until her feet touched the floor. She glanced quickly at the bed that she'd stripped of linen that morning and to her surprise saw the mattress was covered by shiny golden sheets.

"Satin sheets!" she cried. "How decadent. And how sure of yourself you were."

She expected a quick comeback but instead he cupped her head in his hands and gazed at her. "I wasn't sure at all. I only know I want you more than I've ever wanted anything or anyone."

The love she felt for Justin filled her so completely she knew it must be shining from her eyes. She longed to pour out the words of love that welled into her throat but she held them back, afraid the moment would be destroyed if she spoke.

To her, love meant commitment and he hadn't given her any. If she told him how she felt he might not want to hear it, might be turned off completely.

"Oh, God, Alida, those velvet eyes of yours promise so much." His voice was hoarse. "I can't get my bearings, I'm lost. It's like being in the submersible down on the ocean floor. Everything is distorted through hundreds of feet of blue sea water—wonderful beyond description but disorienting. I can map the ocean floor, but I can't chart what's between us."

His hands left her face and lightly, delicately, he traced the curves of her body, his fingers coming back to unbutton her shirt slowly, deliberately. He slid it from her shoulders, then unhooked her wisp of a bra. When her breasts were freed, she heard him catch his breath, but he didn't touch them. Instead, he dropped his hands to his sides.

A moment passed before she realized what he wanted. Her fingers trembled as she started undoing the buttons of his shirt. She had to stretch to ease the shirt off his broad shoulders.

His eyes gleamed as he reached for the fastening of her skirt, released it and pulled it down until it fell around her ankles. When he slipped two fingers under her sheer, brief underpants, his touch seared through her like lightning.

His stomach muscles contracted as she unhooked the clasp of his pants and unzipped them. He groaned when she pulled down his shorts, releasing his aroused manhood. He stepped out of his clothes and slipped off his shoes.

She bent to unfasten her sandals but he stopped her. Kneeling in front of her, he took her shoes off. His thumbs stroked her instep, before his hands traveled up her legs in a slow, delicious journey. Gently but insistently, he eased her thighs apart until his tongue tasted the essence of her womanhood.

She gasped as a quivering began deep within her, an erotic pulsing that left her weak and breathless. When he pulled away from her, she would have fallen if he hadn't held her to him.

"Justin," she moaned.

He lifted her onto the bed, lying close but not quite touching her. Her hands fluttered over the curls of his chest, following the vee down his stomach to the golden cluster of hair below. When she caressed his manhood he murmured inarticulate sounds of pleasure.

Her mouth followed her hands, down, down, his hair crisp under her lips, his skin satiny. The intoxicating odor of his masculinity made the blood pound in her head as she reached his arousal.

"Oh, God," he moaned, pulling her up until she lay atop him, breast to breast.

She looked into golden eyes darkened by passion, by his need for her. Her own need throbbed through her, making her wriggle her hips against him. She bent her head and traced his lips with the tip of her tongue until they opened to welcome her in a consuming, ravenous kiss.

His hands stroked the sides of her breasts, slid down and along the curve of her buttocks. They came back to her shoulders and lifted her so his mouth could reach her nipples, one, then the other, his tongue and lips a rapturous torment.

Nothing existed except Justin, his lips, his hands, his body. The fire of his lovemaking invaded every cell of her body with flaming passion, she was molten with overwhelming desire.

Raising her hips, she fitted herself over his hardness, uttering sounds of delight as she felt him invade her eager softness, plunging deep inside her.

His arms tightened, holding her to him and he rolled over, still joined to her, until she was beneath him. She arched to him in the urgent rhythm of consummation. His lips moved over her face, his tongue warm and caressing.

"Please," she moaned as he thrust gently, slowly within her, the sweet motion driving her into a frenzy of need.

His rhythm increased, he plunged within her, his control abandoned. She writhed beneath him, carried past the boundaries of the known into an unexplored realm of love until she suddenly flared into electric ecstasy, a bolt of lightning flaming across the heavens, she and Justin together in fiery brilliance, their storms of passion released.

Twelve

Alida dreamed she was searching for Justin along dark echoing corridors where the dust lay thick, opening one door after another and finding nothing but empty rooms. She came to a locked door and banged her fists against it, calling his name.

From inside the room came a woman's laughter, high and tinkling. Dread struck her. Priscilla!

"I have him and I'll never let him go," Priscilla said mockingly. "Never-r-r...."

Alida sat up in bed, her heart pounding, a cry of protest rising in her throat. The night-light illuminated the bedroom with a faint glow. Justin was not in the bed or in the room.

"Justin!" she screamed.

She heard running feet, he burst into the bedroom and she reached for him. He sat on the bed, holding her close.

"What's the matter, sweetheart?" he murmured.

"I dreamed I couldn't find you."

"I'm here." His fingers stroked the side of her breast.

Alida pulled away a little. "You're dressed," she accused. "You were leaving without saying good-bye."

"I'd never do that. Lady and I were going to check out the rest of the house." As he mentioned her name, the cat leaped onto the bed and brushed against Alida, her fur soft and tickly against Alida's bare skin.

"I'll come too," she said.

"No, you stay here. I might even change my mind and stay with you." His hand cupped her breast, his thumb rubbing across her nipple. "Mmmm, you feel so good. The house can wait."

She raised her lips to his and lost herself in the sweet magic of his kiss. Moments later he was beside her, his clothes on the floor. Alida fitted herself to him, breast to breast, thigh to thigh, knowing she could never have enough of Justin. What was there to compare to the wonder of his kiss, the glory of his body against hers, the marvel of his caresses?

As their passion rose and the rhythm of their love-making crescendoed, Alida smiled to hear Lady, who'd been trying to sleep on the bed, mew in protest and jump to the floor. Then Justin's fiery ardor claimed her and she no longer heard nor felt anything except the passion binding them together.

She lay in his arms in the afterglow, her head on his chest, listening to the rapid thrum of his heart gradually slow to a resting beat in a reassuring lullaby. She closed her eyes and slept.

It was still dark when Alida felt Justin shift away from her. She came awake instantly to see him easing from the bed.

"No you don't," she told him. "If you're going to search the mansion, you're not leaving me behind. What do you think you'll find, anyway?"

"Nothing. Just a precaution. I'd rather you stayed here, though."

"Why? I'll feel safer with you."

"Stubborn," he muttered.

Alida pulled on jeans and a T-shirt while Justin was dressing. She had her lantern in hand by the time he was ready. When he opened the door to the foyer, Lady darted through, eager to explore with them.

The powerful beam of Justin's big flashlight lit one after another of the empty downstairs rooms. They came back to the foyer where he flashed the light up the staircase.

"Careful now, watch your step," he warned.

Alida smiled. "The day I arrived here and you accosted me in the library, I felt as though you hoped I'd break my neck while you showed me through the house."

His warm fingers massaged her nape. "Wrong. Oh, I'll admit I was furious when I heard an intruder in the library. I rushed in full of righteous wrath, but then you turned and looked at me." He put his arm around her and pulled her close to his side. "A strange sensation rocked me. It was as though I'd always known you from some other life or lives, and now you were standing before me in this one." He grinned ruefully. "And I don't even believe in reincarnation."

"You might have subconsciously recognized me as the little girl who dogged your footsteps sixteen years before."

He shook his head. "I don't deny that may have been mixed in. What I felt, though, was more than seeing the little girl in the beautiful woman she'd become. What I felt shook me so much I was only half-aware of anything I said or did while I was with you. In the attic I damn near took you in my arms. I had to fight myself to keep from doing it."

"You seemed so angry."

"I was." He kissed her forehead, hugging her to him. "It was either hang onto my anger or scare you by trying to make love to you then and there."

"I wonder. If you would have frightened me, I mean."

"So you felt it, too. I suspected you did from the way you looked at me."

"I don't know what I felt. I recognized you almost immediately and, well, I may as well admit that to me at ten you were as godlike as Apollo and just as unattainable. Here you were sixteen years later and I was sixteen years older and . . ." Her words trailed off and she sighed.

"And you wanted me a bit differently than a ten-year-old would. Right?" He smiled at her.

I loved you still, she said to herself, with the love of a woman instead of a girl.

He kissed her with bone-melting tenderness, then put her firmly away from him. "This is what I was afraid would happen if I brought you along. You know I can't keep from touching you."

Alida pointed to the staircase. "Excelsior!"

"As I recall Longfellow's poem, the boy bearing that banner froze to death at the summit. It's a cinch that won't happen tonight."

"Your father and Margaret say this July reminds them of the year Stuart disappeared—hot, the locusts shrilling. And this is the very same night."

"Every July is hot and many summers have had locusts. Tonight is our night, Alida, this isn't the past."

No. And yet hadn't she arrived at the mansion like Priscilla, upsetting everyone, distracting Justin from the woman he wanted to marry?

Justin started up the stairs. His flashlight beam caught Lady halfway up, her eyes gleaming red. A quick search of the upstairs satisfied Justin that the second floor was as empty as the first. He shot his light up the attic stairs, told her to wait below, climbed up enough steps to sweep the attic with his flashlight and returned to her.

"Nothing."

Before they descended to the first floor, Justin drew her into Stuart's room and, opening the french doors to the balcony, lingered in the doorway to let the night breeze cool them.

"Can't we go out onto the balcony?" she asked.

"Too dangerous. The wood's rotten."

Alida, close to him, secure in his embrace, gazed at the darkness of the trees and, far below, the lights of Persis.

Katydids and frogs sang to the full moon that silvered the grounds. The scent of pine mingled with a faint flower sweetness. Alida wished she could wrap up the night as it was at this moment, with Justin beside her, and carry it back to Arizona with her to be savored in the days and weeks to come.

No. This was now. Nothing else existed. Or mattered.

A sound broke into the animal-insect chorus, the mournful rise and fall of the Persis fire whistle.

Justin tensed. "They had a couple of firemen injured the other day. They're going to be short-handed and will need me. I've got to go into town, sweetheart, but I'll be back as soon as I can."

She remembered how he helped out as a volunteer fireman when he visited Persis and smiled, thinking of the boy whose ambition had been to fight fires. "Go ahead. I'll be fine here—we know the house is empty."

"Just the same, I want you locked in the apartment before I go."

Alida meant to stay behind the bolted doors until Justin's return, but he'd no sooner driven away than she realized they'd forgotten Lady. Listening, she fancied she could hear the cat wailing from somewhere above her head.

"Drat it Lady, you certainly can be a problem," she muttered as she pulled back the bolt on the door to the foyer.

Lady didn't come when she called her. Alida tried in vain to remember if she and Justin had closed the door to Stuart's room. Well, the only way to find out if the cat was trapped there was to go up and look. Lantern in her hand, she climbed the stairs.

The door was closed. Alida went in but she didn't see Lady in the room. The balcony, she thought. Sure enough, Lady peered at her through the dusty panes of the closed french doors that led to the balcony. Opening one of the doors, she picked up the cat.

I should have stood up here and waved to Justin as he drove off, she told herself. Balconies were definitely romantic. Except that this one was unsafe and Justin hadn't let her set foot on it.

This balcony was where Stuart had been when David rushed off to find out where the fire was. David hadn't looked back. What would he have seen if he did? Stuart, alone, watching him. Or perhaps someone joining Stuart. Priscilla?

Alida shook her head. Forget the past, Justin had said, and he was right. Somehow, though, it haunted her. The triangle formed by Justin and Renée and her paralleled the old one of Stuart and Margaret and Priscilla.

What would happen?

She sighed. Stuart may have run off with Priscilla, but Justin wasn't likely to run off with her. And would it be right if he did? He must love Renée or he'd never have asked her to marry him.

Lady squirmed in her arms and she stroked the cat, crooning to her. "All right, pretty girl, we'll go downstairs and wait for Justin, don't be so impatient."

Alida's hand was on the doorknob, ready to pull the balcony door shut when she froze, staring into the moonlit night. A dark figure limped toward the front door.

Mrs. Danford? Impossible. She was in the hospital's ICU, seriously ill. Yet it looked like the old woman.

She slammed the door shut and hurried from Stuart's room toward the stairs. Before she reached the bottom, the front door opened. The rays of Alida's lantern illuminated a nightmare face. She gasped.

Mrs. Danford lurched into the foyer, gray hair wild about her ashen face, breath rasping in her throat. For an instant Alida was ten again, terror stricken at the thought of facing the wicked old witch from Hansel and Gretel.

Lady spat, leaped from her grasp and fled toward the still open door to the apartment. Alida pulled herself together.

"Mrs. Danford, you shouldn't have left the hospital," she said, trying to convince herself she wasn't afraid of this tottering, obviously sick old woman.

"You!" Mrs. Danford, cried, lunging at Alida. The lantern's beam gleamed on the steel secateurs in her hand.

Alida, standing on the second step, started to dodge away as the sharp shears thrust at her. But her foot slipped and she fell, sliding helplessly down to sprawl on her back at Mrs. Danford's feet.

The old woman gazed down malevolently as Alida tried desperately to scramble away. Mrs. Danford bent over, her arm rose, the secateurs in her hand, too close for Alida to escape. Her mouth opened to scream.

Mrs. Danford stopped short. The weapon dropped from her hand to thud onto the parquet floor next to Alida's head. Alida scrambled to her feet, retrieved the secateurs, ready to run until she saw that Mrs. Danford was paying no attention to her.

The old woman watched the dark at the head of the stairs, her mouth working. She swayed from side to side, one hand clutching at her chest. "Stuart!" she cried. Her voice dropped to a hoarse whisper. "Stuart..." She fell forward onto her knees, then slid to the floor and began gasping for breath.

Warily, Alida approached her. Mrs. Danford's eyes were still fixed on the stairs. Alida glanced quickly toward them, seeing nothing but darkness.

"Stuart's waiting for me," the old woman gasped. "He's standing at the top of the stairs, waiting."

Alida stared at her, mind whirling in confusion. Stuart? What did Mrs. Danford have to do with Stuart McLeod? Flicking uneasy glances toward the stairs, she eased onto her knees beside the old woman.

"Don't you hear him calling me?" Mrs. Danford asked, each word a painful effort. "'Priscilla,' that's what he's saying. 'I know you, Priscilla, you can't fool me with gray hair and wrinkles.'"

Alida jerked back in disbelief. Priscilla? Mrs. Danford was Priscilla? Her mind must be wandering.

"You're very ill," Alida said. "I'll drive down to your house and call an ambulance. You need—"

"Too late. No ambulance. Stuart is calling me and I must go."

Alida leaned forward. "You—you're really Priscilla Tudor?"

Mrs. Danford ignored the question. "I tried to scare you away, but you wouldn't go," she muttered. "You meddled, you found my diary. And I saw him kissing you, it was you he wanted. Just like Stuart, he's Stuart all over again. That's why I set the fire."

"What fire?" Alida whispered.

"At the house," Mrs. Danford said. "At her house. She was winning, after all, and had to be punished. I hated her. Stuart was mine...." Her eyes drooped shut.

She's got me confused with Margaret and Justin with Stuart, Alida thought. That's why she tried to kill me.

"They all rushed to the fire. All except Stuart." Mrs. Danford's voice was so faint Alida had to bend closer to hear her. "I went to Stuart's room. He pushed me away. Said he was going to Margaret. Loved her, not me. Not true." The dark eyes opened. "I ran after him to the stairs. He looked back at me. I saw disgust in his eyes. I shoved him hard. He fell. Down the stairs. Died. No one home. Old wagon in the shed. Lifted him." Tears streaked her withered cheeks. "He was still beautiful dead. Then I ran away. My life...many men. I suffered." Her gaze went past Alida to the stairs. "I loved only Stuart. Now he's waiting, at last he's waiting for me."

Alida swallowed, scarcely able to take in what she'd heard. Had Priscilla killed Stuart all those years ago because he'd rejected her?

Mrs. Danford's eyes closed again and her breathing changed, becoming less gasping, weaker. She muttered something inaudible and Alida put her ear to the old woman's lips.

"The roses," Mrs. Danford whispered. "My beautiful red roses. For him." She sighed and her breathing ceased altogether.

Alida felt for a pulse, couldn't find one, gingerly laid her ear against Mrs. Danford's chest but heard no heart beat.

Priscilla was dead.

Alida sat back on her heels, tears in her eyes. So many wasted lives. Stuart's, Margaret's—Priscilla's, too. Only a terrible life could have changed her from a pretty young girl into an old woman before she was sixty.

But, oh, the havoc Priscilla had caused. She'd burned the Randolph's home, killed Stuart, and left Margaret and the McLeods with the burden of never knowing what had happened on that July twenty-sixth. How Stuart's parents must have hoped and prayed he'd return home someday. And all the time he was dead. Dead and hidden somewhere on the estate, probably in the woods. Alida shuddered.

Slowly she rose, entered the apartment and brought out a blanket. Gently she laid it over Priscilla's still figure. What Priscilla had done was wrong, evil. And, Alida now knew, she had tried to harm her as well, first with the rag fire, then by trying to push her down the stairs as she'd pushed Stuart, finally tonight with the secateurs. Priscilla would never harm anyone again.

Alida eyed the covered figure. "Rest in peace," she whispered.

The morning of Mrs. Danford's funeral dawned bright and clear. A thunderstorm the night before had cooled the air and the day promised to be pleasant. Alida stood in the doorway of her motel. It wasn't the best Persis had to offer, but it allowed her to have Lady. She breathed deeply of the soft summer air.

Alida felt she should stay on until Priscilla was buried. And, if she was absolutely honest, she'd have to admit she longed to see Justin just once more before she left the Catskills.

When Justin had gone to his father with the complete story of Priscilla's identity and terrible deeds, David collapsed and had to be rushed to the Persis hospital. As soon as he was conscious, David insisted on being flown to Boston in an air ambulance so his own doctor could care for him. Naturally, Justin had gone with his father.

Justin called her from Boston saying David was improving but wouldn't be able to return for the funeral. Justin intended to try to attend.

If he did, she'd see Justin today. For the last time.

As for the sale of the McLeod estate, David had signed the papers before his collapse. There were no problems except for the gatehouse property, and KHI would be able to buy that from Mrs. Danford's estate. Alida had accomplished what she'd been sent here to do.

Unfortunately, her success didn't mean as much to her as it should. On the jet flying in to New York, she'd been so certain nothing would delight her more than tying up the McLeod deal and returning to Phoenix in triumph.

How wrong she'd been.

Of course she was pleased the sale had gone through, but her success did nothing to relieve the leaden weight in her chest. It seemed to grow heavier and heavier every time she thought about leaving Justin.

She fantasized about him coming to her, taking her in his arms and saying she was his one true love, that he wanted to spend the rest of his life with her. She knew it was a scene that wouldn't be played out in real life. And yet she couldn't help fanning a glimmer of hope.

Lady mewed unhappily from her carrier, and Alida turned back to the room. She was taking no chances on the cat escaping again, but Lady couldn't understand that. All she knew was she wanted out of the carrier. Now.

"Poor kitty, you have a few more bad hours to go through before I get you home to Phoenix," Alida said. "You'll like Phoenix, I promise you. You'll be happy there."

But *I* won't, she thought. Will I ever be happy again?

A last check in the mirror told her the dark blue silk suit and linen shirt was in good taste for a funeral. It certainly matched her mood.

Leaving the cat and her packed bags in the motel room, Alida started off for the Ferndale Cemetery where a short graveside service was to be held. On the way, she passed a fire-gutted tavern and realized it must be what had burned the night Priscilla died. With all that had happened she'd forgotten until this moment why Justin had left her alone in the house that night.

The cemetery was around the next curve. Alida pulled into the driveway, parked, and walked up a rise, then stopped, drawing in her breath.

Justin stood only yards away from her, talking to the minister. Her heart trebled its beat as she hurried to him, barely able to keep herself from running.

"Alida!" His eyes glowed and his smile warmed her as he took her hand.

As he introduced her to the Episcopal minister, Alida heard Margaret Randolph calling her name. Moments later Margaret stood beside them.

"I told David I had to fly back for the funeral," she said to Alida. "I wanted to be here for both of us, to at last make an ending." Her face had lost its permanent set of sadness, making her look younger and more attractive. "I'll be returning to Boston to stay with David until he's completely recovered," she added.

Alida wondered if, in Margaret's place, she'd have been able to attend the funeral of the woman who'd killed the man she loved. Maybe Margaret was right, though, in coming. Perhaps she sought to end the past before she and David began to plan for the future. A future together? The thought eased her own unhappiness.

The minister said a brief prayer, recited an abbreviated funeral service, and was giving a final benediction when brakes squealed and a car door slammed. Ignoring the noise, he finished and shook Justin's hand.

Alida, looking toward the parking area, saw Renée striding toward the grave, stunning in a black dress, her blond hair swinging.

Justin, turning to Alida, didn't notice Renée's approach. "I'll meet you at the motel later," he said. "There's something I have to take care of and then—"

Seeing that Margaret had intercepted Renée and was talking to her, Alida spoke quickly. "I'm leaving for New York City immediately. I'm through here and overdue in Phoenix. There's really nothing to keep me in Persis any longer."

He stared at her. "We need to talk. I want you to wait for me."

"I'm not Priscilla." Alida kept her voice low. "I won't repeat the past; I won't come between you and Renée."

"Between me and Renée? What the hell is the matter with—?"

"Justin!" Renée cried, deftly separating Alida from him by stepping between them. "I've been so worried about David. Margaret tells me he's better—is that true?"

Alida turned and walked rapidly away. In her heart of hearts she nourished a tiny flame of hope. Justin would run after her, take her in his arms...

No. Renée would see that didn't happen.

At the motel Alida loaded her bags and Lady into the car, noticing that Thunder Mountain was again collecting storm clouds above its summit. On the way to the main highway that would take her to the city, she had to pass the turnoff to the McLeod mansion.

Impulsively she swung the car onto the Thunder Mountain road and began to climb.

This is stupid, she argued. You're wasting time. But she drove on until she reached the gatehouse. She stopped at the chain and got out of the car, the scent of the roses heavy about her. Already some of the blossoms were past their prime and needed to be cut off, but Priscilla would never behead faded flowers with her sharp secateurs again. No one was left to take care of Priscilla's roses.

Alida picked a rose that was about to unfurl, one of the reddest, as red as blood. She brought it into the car, the petals silky under her fingers.

What do you intend to do with the rose? she asked herself as she drove down the mountain. Bring it back to Phoenix and press it in a book until it's withered, the scent faded? A sad memento to mourn over?

Keep going now, don't stop again to do anything else foolish. Your time here is done. Over.

But near the reservoir she thought she recognized the spot where Justin had stopped the day he'd taken her on the picnic. Before she was aware of what she intended, she'd parked the car off the road and was searching for the break in the wire fence, the rose still in her hand.

When she reached the rocky point she stared down at the still water where once she'd seen a reflection of herself with Justin. This time she stood alone, the red of the rose dark in the blue water. A beautiful red rose. . . .

Suddenly hair pricked on the back of her neck. The roses. Priscilla's last words about the roses. "For Stuart," she'd said and now Alida was afraid she understood what Priscilla had meant.

Stuart wasn't buried in some hidden grave in the woods. No, Priscilla had somehow hauled him in the wagon all the way down to the gatehouse and buried him there in the soft soil where drain pipes for a septic tank had been laid and covered over that very day.

That's why Priscilla had come back. To plant rose bushes as a memorial to the man whose favorite flower they'd been. To plant the roses and to tend them and her love, buried under her beautiful red roses.

With a convulsive gesture, Alida flung the rose into the water. As it drifted away she made a vow.

If she voiced her suspicions, David and Margaret, who'd been hurt enough already, would surely suffer all over again. The past was better off left buried. She'd let Stuart stay asleep under the roses.

She'd keep Priscilla's last secret.

Thirteen

Slowly and sadly, Alida walked back to the car. She could no longer put off leaving, she had to go. Her head told her she was doing the right thing, though her heart ached with longing.

All that Justin had ever said to her echoed in her mind. Just remembering his husky voice when he murmured her name as they made love sent a thrill along her legs.

All the warmth of the sun was in his eyes; what would warm her when she was no longer near him? A tear trickled down her cheek and she wiped it away impatiently.

Don't cry. You have a long drive ahead. Stop indulging yourself.

I don't want to leave him, her heart insisted. I can't bear the loss.

You will, you will. You'll survive.

Like Margaret? she thought bitterly. Living half a life?

At least now Margaret had the consolation of knowing Stuart had truly loved her, had chosen her above all other women. But did that make up for all she'd missed through the years?

She caught sight of the car parked under the pine where she'd left it. Something about it looked wrong and she frowned, increasing her pace. As she neared the car, she blinked in disbelief. The roof and hood were covered with golden flowers. Covered with brown-eyed susans.

Alida stood stock still, afraid to believe what she was seeing. It must be a fantasy. No other car was in sight, no one was by her car. She closed her eyes and opened them again. The flowers were still there.

She whirled around, scanning every bush, every tree. No one. Holding her breath, she advanced toward the car and plucked a brown-eyed susan from the hood. The petals were velvety under her fingers. Real.

Suddenly Justin leaped into sight on the other side of the car and she screamed in shocked surprise.

"Good," he said. "I hope I upset you as much as you did me a little while ago."

She gaped at him. He stared back at her across the flower-strewn hood, his eyes cloudy with anger.

"You're so damn hard-headed, such a conclusion-jumper," he growled. "Did it ever occur to you to ask me if it was *my* ring on Renée's finger? It's not, you didn't get the facts before you made a leaping assumption. Anything between Renée and me was over long ago. We're friends, nothing more."

"On your side, maybe," she said defensively. "I wouldn't bet on Renée."

He shrugged. "She's engaged to a man in Texas. He'll be her second husband, if that matters."

Alida swallowed. "You never once said you loved me."

"Good God, didn't I show you every time I looked at you, every time I touched you?"

"How could I be sure?"

"All right, damn it, I love you!" he shouted. "What the hell ever gave you the notion we were re-enacting the past? I'm not Stuart, you're not Priscilla, and Renée certainly isn't Margaret."

"The past haunted me. Maybe it was because I stayed in the old mansion."

"The past is gone just as the towns in the reservoir are covered by the waters of Esopus. KHI will be tearing down the old McLeod house and then nothing will be left of the past." He stalked around the front of the car and stood over her. "This is our time and I love you. Do you understand?"

Her heart soared with happiness, only one dark strand holding it to earth.

"The gatehouse—" she began.

"Mrs. Danford—Priscilla—willed it to me. That's where I went after the funeral, to see her lawyer. She wanted me to have the gatehouse because she thought I looked like Stuart. I'll sell the place to KHI as fast as I can; I don't want any reminder of the past."

"But her roses—"

He threw his arms in the air. "Damn the roses! If I must, I'll put in a proviso that KHI has to keep the rose garden just as it is now. Does that suit you?"

Slowly, Alida nodded.

His hands closed over her upper arms. "One more item, my elusive little gypsy. How do you expect me to propose to a woman who hasn't yet said how she feels about me?"

"I—" she sputtered, "but I—you must have seen, you must have known . . ."

"I believe you just told me action doesn't take the place of words." His hands slid down to her waist.

She swayed toward him.

Golden eyes alight with amusement, he held her away. "Not until I hear it straight from the gypsy's lips."

"Okay, okay. I lo—"

Lightning sizzled from the clouds atop the mountain and the rumbling boom of thunder drowned her out completely.

They both jumped. Then, holding onto each other, they rocked with laughter.

When he could speak, Justin said, "We can't argue with a pronouncement from the heavens. Obviously fate intended us to fall in love."

Alida pulled his head down. "Who's arguing?" she murmured against his lips before they kissed.

And in the kiss was thunder, lightning, the heavens, and, most wonderful of all, love. Alida knew she'd found her home at last. In Justin's arms.

The Silhouette Cameo Tote Bag Now available for just $6.99

Handsomely designed in blue and bright pink, its stylish good looks make the Cameo Tote Bag an attractive accessory. The Cameo Tote Bag is big and roomy (13″ square), with reinforced handles and a snap-shut top. You can buy the Cameo Tote Bag for $6.99, plus $1.50 for postage and handling.

Send your name and address with check or money order for $6.99 (plus $1.50 postage and handling), a total of $8.49 to:

**Silhouette Books
120 Brighton Road
P.O. Box 5084
Clifton, NJ 07015-5084
ATTN: Tote Bag**

SIL-T-1

The Silhouette Cameo Tote Bag can be purchased pre-paid only. No charges will be accepted. Please allow 4 to 6 weeks for delivery.

Arizona and N.Y. State Residents Please Add Sales Tax

Offer not available in Canada.

Take 4 Silhouette Special Edition novels
FREE
and preview future books in your home for 15 days!

When you take advantage of this offer, you get 4 Silhouette Special Edition® novels FREE and without obligation. Then you'll also have the opportunity to preview 6 brand-new books —delivered right to your door for a FREE 15-day examination period—as soon as they are published.

When you decide to keep them, you pay just $1.95 each ($2.50 each in Canada) *with no shipping, handling, or other charges of any kind!*

Romance *is* alive, well and flourishing in the moving love stories of Silhouette Special Edition novels. They'll awaken your desires, enliven your senses, and leave you tingling all over with excitement...and the first 4 novels are yours to keep. You can cancel at any time.

As an added bonus, you'll also receive a FREE subscription to the Silhouette Books Newsletter as long as you remain a member. Each issue is filled with news on upcoming books, interviews with your favorite authors, even their favorite recipes.

To get your 4 FREE books, fill out and mail the coupon today!

Silhouette Special Edition®

Silhouette Books, 120 Brighton Rd., P.O. Box 5084, Clifton, NJ 07015-5084

Silhouette Desire

COMING NEXT MONTH

OUT OF THIS WORLD—Janet Joyce
When Adrienne met Kendrick, she thought he was an alien from outer space. He insisted he wasn't, but how could she believe him when his mere touch sent her soaring to the heavens?

DESPERADO—Doreen Owens Malek
Half Seminole Indian, Andrew Fox had chosen the dangerous life of a bounty hunter. As a student of Indian folklore, Cindy found him fascinating—as a woman, she found him irresistible.

PICTURE OF LOVE—Robin Elliott
It didn't take Steve long to realize Jade was the woman for him, but Jade was a compulsive overachiever. Could she manage to temper her ambition and make room for love?

SONGBIRD—Syrie A. Astrahan
Desirée had to choose—her career as a disk jockey in California or Kyle Harrison, the man she loved, in Seattle. Could she possibly find the best of both worlds?

BODY AND SOUL—Jennifer Greene
Joel Brannigan fought for what he wanted, and he wanted Dr. Claire Barrett. She was ready for a fair fight, but Joel didn't fight fair...and he always won.

IN THE PALM OF HER HAND—Dixie Browning
Fate had thrown Shea Bellwood and Dave Pendleton together under rather bizarre circumstances, but who can argue with fate—especially when it leads to love.

AVAILABLE NOW:

CAUTIOUS LOVER
Stephanie James

WHEN SNOW MEETS FIRE
Christine Flynn

HEAVEN ON EARTH
Sandra Kleinschmit

NO MAN'S KISSES
Nora Powers

THE SHADOW BETWEEN
Diana Stuart

NOTHING VENTURED
Suzanne Simms